[新装版] ポール・オースターが朗読する
ナショナル・ストーリー・プロジェクト

ポール・オースター 編・朗読
柴田元幸 他・訳

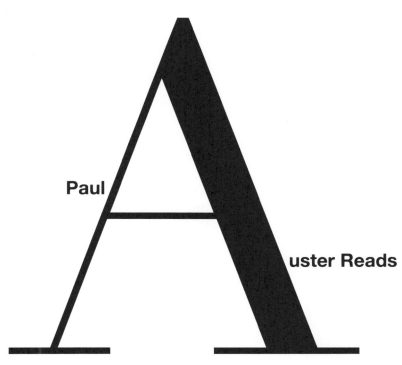

Paul

uster Reads

National Story Project

Paul Auster Reads the National Story Project
ポール・オースターが朗読する
ナショナル・ストーリー・プロジェクト

ポール・オースター 編・朗読
柴田元幸 他・訳

リンダ・エレガント
ジャネット・シュミット・ズーパン
イーディス・ライマー
ロバート・M・ロック
スタン・ベンコスキー
ジョー・ミセリ
ジョーン・ウィルキンズ・ストーン
ジョー・リゾ
キャサリン・オースティン・アレグザンダー
ライオン・グッドマン
ロバート・ウィニー
シオドア・ラスティグ
ロリー・パイコフ
リンダ・マリーン
エレン・パウエル
グレース・フィクテルバーグ
B・C
アメニ・ローザ

装幀　松田行正＋杉本聖士

Editor's Note

Grateful thanks to the following people for their help and support: Daniel Zwerdling, Jacki Lyden, Rebecca Davis, Davar Ardalan, Walter Ray Watson, Kitty Eisele, Marta Haywood, and Hannah Misol — all of *Weekend All Things Considered* — as well as to Carol Mann, Jennifer Barth and — first, last, and always — Siri Hustvedt.

P. A.

編者より

以下の方々のご協力に感謝する。ダニエル・ズワードリング、ジャッキ・ライデン、レベッカ・デイヴィス、ダヴァー・アーダラン、ウォルター・レイ・ワトソン、キティ・アイゼリ、マータ・ヘイウッド、ハンナ・マイソル（以上、『すべてを俎上に　週末版』スタッフ）、キャロル・マン、ジェニファー・バース、そして――最初に、最後に、そしてつねに――シリ・ハストヴェット。

P・A

Contents 目次

英語とアメリカの物語を楽しむ
『ポール・オースターが朗読する ナショナル・ストーリー・プロジェクト』 編集部編 … 008

【無料】英文音声の入手・活用方法　編集部編 … 010

INTRODUCTION 🎧001-021
イントロダクション　ポール・オースター … 011

編訳者まえがき　柴田元幸 … 038

[Story 1] 🎧022-023
ANIMALS
The Chicken
鶏／リンダ・エレガント（オレゴン州ポートランド） … 044

[Story 2] 🎧024-037
ANIMALS
Vertigo
ヴァーティゴ／ジャネット・シュミット・ズーパン（モンタナ州ミズーラ） … 046

[Story 3] 🎧038-047
OBJECTS
A Bicycle Story
自転車物語／イーディス・ライマー（ニューヨーク州チェリーヴァレー） … 060

[Story 4] 🎧048-053
OBJECTS
The Striped Pen
縞の万年筆／ロバート・M・ロック（カリフォルニア州サンタローザ） … 070

[Story 5] 🎧054-058
FAMILIES
Rainout
雨天中止／スタン・ベンコスキー（カリフォルニア州サニーヴェイル）… 078

[Story 6] 🎧059-091
FAMILIES
Taking Leave
別れを告げる／ジョー・ミセリ（ニューヨーク州オーバーン）… 082

[Story 7] 🎧092-096
SLAPSTICK
A Felt Fedora
フェルトの中折れ帽／ジョーン・ウィルキンズ・ストーン（ワシントン州ゴールデンデール）… 108

[Story 8] 🎧097-108
SLAPSTICK
Bronx Cheer
ブロンクス流どたばた／ジョー・リゾ（ニューヨーク州ブロンクス）… 112

[Story 9] 🎧109-113
STRANGERS
Dancing on Seventy-fourth Street
74丁目のダンス／キャサリン・オースティン・アレグザンダー（ワシントン州シアトル）… 122

[Story 10] 🎧114-151
STRANGERS
A Shot in the Light
怪我の「光明」／ライオン・グッドマン（カリフォルニア州サンラファエル）… 126

[Story 11]　🎧152-156
WAR
I Thought My Father Was God
父さんは神様だと思った／ロバート・ウィニー（アイダホ州ボナーズフェリー）… 156

[Story 12]　🎧157-164
LOVE
What If?
もしも／シオドア・ラスティグ（ウェストヴァージニア州モーガンタウン）… 164

[Story 13]　🎧165-178
LOVE
Table for Two
お二人席／ロリー・パイコフ（カリフォルニア州ロサンゼルス）… 170

[Story 14]　🎧179-187
DEATH
I Didn't Know
知らなかった／リンダ・マリーン（ウィスコンシン州ミドルトン）… 182

[Story 15]　🎧188-201
DEATH
Dress Rehearsal
予行演習／エレン・パウエル（ヴァーモント州サウスバーリントン）… 188

[Story 16]　🎧202-208
DREAMS
Heaven
天国／グレース・フィクテルバーグ（ニューメキシコ州ランチョス・デ・タオス）… 202

[Story 17] 🎧209-222
MEDITATIONS
Homeless in Prescott, Arizona
アリゾナ州プレスコットのホームレス／B・C（アリゾナ州プレスコット） … 212

[Story 18] 🎧223-238
MEDITATIONS
An Average Sadness
ありきたりな悲しみ／アメニ・ローザ（マサチューセッツ州ウィリアムズタウン） … 222

Spoken Introductions to the Stories
ポール・オースターによる物語紹介 … 232

What's "Paul Auster Reads the National Story Project"?
『ポール・オースターが朗読するナショナル・ストーリー・プロジェクト』とは？ … 236

英語とアメリカの物語を楽しむ
『ポール・オースターが朗読する ナショナル・ストーリー・プロジェクト』
編集部編／柴田元幸監修

　本書『ポール・オースターが朗読するナショナル・ストーリー・プロジェクト』は、ラジオ番組に投稿された「アメリカの物語」を、❶原文、❷翻訳、❸朗読、といろいろな角度から味わうことで英語が学べます。ここでは、本書で英語力をアップさせる方法を目的別にお教えします。

[楽しみ方　その1]
リーディング：物語を英語で読む
左ページには原文の英語を掲載しています。英語の原書を読んだことのない人も、右ページの訳やページ下の脚注を頼りに英語のリーディングに挑戦してみましょう。本書掲載の物語は比較的平易な英語で書かれているので、読みやすく感じるはずです。自信がついたら、原書の小説に挑戦してみては？

[楽しみ方　その2]
リスニング：物語の朗読を聞く
本書には、編者であるポール・オースターによる英語の朗読を用意しています。意味の固まりを意識しながら聞くと、英語の構文の感覚を養えるでしょう。何度も繰り返し聞くことで、英語のリズムやイントネーションに慣れ、リスニング力がアップします。

[楽しみ方　その3]
リピーティング：朗読を聴いて繰り返し言ってみる
リピーティングとは1センテンスごとに音声を止め、聞こえたままにまねをして、感情を込めて英語を口に出すことです。最初から全部をリピーティングするのではなく、お気に入りのパラグラフ（段落）を選んで取り組むとよいでしょう。英語をしっかりと聞き取ることでリスニング力、そして、忠実に再生することで話し方のリズムやイントネーションを身に付けられるのでスピーキング力アップに役立ちます。

[楽しみ方　その4]
ディクテーション：朗読の英語を書き取る
朗読の音声を繰り返し聞いて、英語を書き取ります。聞いて書き取ることによって現在の英語力を認識することができます。集中して英語を聞くのでリスニング力が伸び、英語が頭に残るのでスピーキングにも活きてきます。リピーティング同様、覚えてしまいたいくらいに気に入った1パラグラフから始めるのがよいでしょう。

[楽しみ方　その5]
トランスレーション：物語を日本語に訳す
左ページに英語、右ページに翻訳という対訳形式になっていますので、翻訳者がいかに英語を日本語に置き換えているかを読み比べることが可能です。物語を翻訳し、自訳と掲載された訳とを較べて添削することによって、より深く英語のニュアンスを理解し味わうことができます。

【無料】英文音声の入手・活用方法　編集部編

本書の英文音声は、以下の要領で無料でダウンロードしていただけます。
本サービスのご利用には、メールアドレスIDの登録／ログインが必要となります（無料）。あらかじめご了承ください。

パソコンの場合

パソコンで、音声データをダウンロードするには、以下のURLから行います。

1) アルクのダウンロードセンター
   https://www.alc.co.jp/dl/
2) ログイン後、ダウンロードセンターで、書籍名または商品コード 7019061 でコンテンツを検索します。
3) 検索後、ダウンロード用ボタンをクリックし、以下のパスワードを入力してコンテンツをダウンロードしてください。

スマートフォンの場合

スマートフォンまたはiPadに直接ダウンロードするには、無料アプリ「語学のオトモ ALCO」が必要です（ALCOインストール済みの方は3から）。iOS、Androidの両方に対応しています。再生スピードの変更や、秒数指定の巻き戻し・早送りなど、便利な機能が満載です。語学学習にぜひご活用ください。

1) ALCOのインストール
   https://www.alc.co.jp/alco/
2) インストール後、ALCOへのログインには、メールアドレスIDの登録が必要となります（無料）。
3) ALCOにログインし、ホーム画面の下部にある「ダウンロードセンター」バーをタップします（QRコードを使えば、以下4、5の操作が不要です）。
4) ダウンロードセンターで、書籍名または商品コード 7019061 でコンテンツを検索します。
5) 検索後、ダウンロード用ボタンをクリックし、以下のパスワードを入力します。個別ダウンロードページから、コンテンツをダウンロードしてください。

　　パスワード　→　auster61

※サービスの内容は、予告なく変更する場合がございます。あらかじめご了承ください。

🎧 001-021

INTRODUCTION

イントロダクション

🎧002

I never intended to do this. The *National Story Project* came about by accident, and ❶if not for a remark my wife made at the dinner table sixteen months ago, most of the pieces in this book never would have been written. It was May 1999, perhaps June, and earlier that day I had been interviewed on ❷National Public Radio about my most recent novel. After we finished our conversation, Daniel Zwerdling, the host of ❸*Weekend All Things Considered*, had asked me if I would be interested in becoming a regular ❹contributor to the program. I couldn't even see his face when he asked the question. I was in the NPR studio on Second Avenue in New York, and he was in Washington, D.C. For the past twenty or thirty minutes we had been talking to each other through microphones and headsets, aided by a technological marvel known as ❺fiber optics. I asked him what he had in mind, and he said that he wasn't sure. Maybe I could come on the air every month or so and tell stories.

🎧003

I wasn't interested. Doing my own work was difficult enough, and taking on a job that would force me to ❻crank out stories ❼on command was ❽the last thing I needed. But, just to be polite, I said that I would go home and think about it.

It was my wife, ❾Siri, who turned the proposition on its head. That night, when I told her about NPR's curious offer, she imme-

---

※トラック001をはじめ、オースターによる導入のナレーションのスクリプトは、232〜235ページにまとめて掲載されています。
❶if not for ...: もし〜がなければ　❷National Public Radio: 全米公共ラジオ（非営利ラジオ局の全米ネットワーク。資金の一部は公共放送協会を通じて国の予算から出る）　❸*Weekend All Things Considered*:『すべてを俎上に　週末版』(「万事を考慮すれば」という常套句を番組名に使っている)　❹contributor: 参加者、出演者　❺fiber optics: 光ファイバー　❻crank out ...: 〜をひ

私としてはこんなことをするつもりはなかった。『ナショナル・ストーリー・プロジェクト』は偶然から生まれたのだ。1年4カ月ばかり前に私の妻が夕食の席で発した一言がなかったら、この本に収められた文章の大半は書かれることもなく終わっていただろう。1999年5月だったか、あるいは6月だったかもしれない。その日の昼、私はNPR(全米公共ラジオ)に出演して、最新作についてインタビューを受けた。インタビューが済むと、『すべてを俎上に　週末版』のホストを務めているダニエル・ズワードリングから、番組のレギュラーになる気はないかと訊かれた。そう訊かれたとき、私にはダニエルの顔すら見えていなかった。こちらはニューヨークの二番街にあるNPRのスタジオに、あちらはワシントンDCにいて、それまでの20分か30分、我々はマイクとヘッドホンを通し、光ファイバーなるテクノロジーの驚異に助けられて喋っていたのである。どういうものを考えていらっしゃるんです、と訊くと、いやべつにこれというアイデアはないんですとダニエルは言った。たとえば月に一度くらい出ていただいて、物語を語っていただくというのはどうでしょうね。

　惹かれる話ではなかった。何しろ自分の仕事をするだけでも精一杯なのだ。他人の要請に応じて定期的に物語をひねり出すなんて、できるわけがない。だがまあいちおう礼儀もあるし、帰って少し考えてみますと答えておいた。

　この提案を180度ひっくり返してみせたのが妻のシリである。その晩、NPRの奇妙な誘いを口にすると、シリはすぐさま、私の考えの方向

ねり出す　❼on command: 注文を受けて　❽the last thing I needed: 私がもっとも必要としていないもの＝絶対お断りのもの　❾Siri: 本書の編者オースターの妻、シリ・ハストヴェット(Siri Hustvedt)。1955年生まれの作家。作品に、*The Blindfold*(1992: 邦題『目かくし』[白水社])、*What I Loved*(2003)などがある

イントロダクション　013

diately came up with a proposal that reversed the direction of my thoughts. In a matter of thirty seconds, no had become yes.

You don't have to write the stories yourself, she said. Get people to sit down and write their own stories. They could send them in to you, and then you could read the best ones on the radio. If enough people wrote in, it can turn into something extraordinary.

That was how the *National Story Project* was born. It was Siri's idea, and then I picked it up and started to run with it.

🎧 004

Sometime in late September, Zwerdling came to my house in ❶Brooklyn with Rebecca Davis, one of the producers of *Weekend All Things Considered*, and we ❷launched the idea of the project in the form of another interview. I told the listeners that I was looking for stories. The stories had to be true, and they had to be short, but there would be no restrictions as to subject matter or style. What interested me most, I said, were stories that ❸defied our expectations about the world, ❹anecdotes that revealed the mysterious and unknowable forces at work in our lives, in our family histories, in our minds and bodies, in our souls. In other words, true stories that sounded like fiction. I was talking about big things and small things, tragic things and comic things, any experience that felt important enough to set down on paper. They shouldn't worry if they had never written a story, I said. Everyone was bound to know

---

❶Brooklyn: ブルックリン（ニューヨーク市の区のひとつ）　❷launch:（新しい計画など）を世に送り出す　❸defy:（理解や予測）を超える、絶する　❹anecdote: 逸話、エピソード

を逆転させる新提案を思いついたのである。30秒のあいだに、ノーはイエスに変わっていた。

　あなたが物語を書くことはないのよ、とシリは言った。いろんな人にそれぞれ自分の物語を書いてもらえばいいのよ。リスナーの人たちから送ってもらって、一番いいやつをあなたが番組で朗読するのよ。それなりの数が集まったら、ひょっとするとすごい番組になるかも。

　こうしてナショナル・ストーリー・プロジェクトは生まれた。それはシリのアイデアだったのであり、私はそれを受けて走り出したのである。

　9月末にズワードリングが、『すべてを俎上に』のプロデューサーの一人レベッカ・デイヴィスを連れてブルックリンのわが家を訪ねてきた。今回もインタビューという形を使って、我々はプロジェクトのアイデアを世に送り出した。物語を求めているのです、と私は聴取者に呼びかけた。物語は事実でなければならず、短くないといけませんが、内容やスタイルに関しては何ら制限はありません。私が何より惹かれるのは、世界とはこういうものだという私たちの予想をくつがえす物語であり、私たちの家族の歴史のなか、私たちの心や体、私たちの魂のなかで働いている神秘にして知りがたいさまざまな力を明かしてくれる逸話なのです。言いかえれば、作り話のように聞こえる実話。大きな事柄でもいいし小さな事柄でもいいし、悲劇的な話、喜劇的な話、とにかく紙に書きつけたいという気になるほど大切に思えた体験なら何でもいいのです。いままで物語なんて一度も書いたことがなくても心配は要りません。人

some good ones, and if enough people answered the call to participate, we would inevitably begin to learn some surprising things about ourselves and each other. The spirit of the project was entirely democratic. All listeners were welcome to ❶contribute, and I promised to read every story that came in. People would be exploring their own lives and experiences, but at the same time they would be part of a collective effort, something bigger than just themselves. With their help, I said, I was hoping to ❷put together an ❸archive of facts, a museum of American reality.

🎧 005

The interview was broadcast on the first Saturday in October, 1999, and since then, I have received more than five thousand ❹submissions. This number is many times greater than what I had ❺anticipated, and since the beginning, I have been ❻awash in manuscripts, floating madly in an ever expanding sea of paper. Some of the stories are written by hand; others are typed; still others are printed out from e-mails. Every month, I have ❼scrambled to choose five or six of the best ones and turn them into a twenty-minute ❽segment to be aired on *Weekend All Things Considered*. It has been singularly rewarding work, one of the most inspiring tasks I have ever undertaken. But it has had its difficult moments as well. On several occasions, when I have been particularly ❾swamped with material, I have read sixty or seventy stories at a single ❿sitting, and each time I have done that, I have stood up

---

❶contribute: 投稿する ❷put together . . .: 〜を作り上げる ❸archive: アーカイブ（本来は文書を保管した場所のこと） ❹submission: 投稿 ❺anticipate: 〜を予想する ❻(be) awash in . . .: 〜に浸る ❼scramble to do: あわただしく〜する ❽segment:（放送などの）一番組、一本 ❾(be) swamped with . . .: 〜で圧倒される ❿sitting:（座って中断せずに行う）一仕事

はみな、面白い話をいくつか知っているものなのですから。この呼びかけに十分な数の人が応じてくれたら、きっとそれは、自分やたがいについて驚くべき事実を知る絶好の機会となるにちがいありません。このプロジェクトの精神は100パーセント民主的です。どなたからの投稿も歓迎します。送られてきた物語は私がすべて目を通します、と私は約束した。一人ひとりが自分の人生や経験を探るわけですが、と同時に、それによって誰もが、ひとつの集合的な企て、自分一人より大きな何かに加わることになるのです。みなさんに協力していただいて、事実のアーカイブを、アメリカの現実の博物館を作れたらと思っているのです。

　このインタビューが1999年10月の第一土曜日に放送され、それ以来、5000通を越える投稿を私は受けとった。予想をはるかに上回る数字だ。スタート以来、私は原稿の波間に漂って過ごし、ますます広がっていく紙の海に狂おしく浮かんできた。手書きの原稿もあればタイプ原稿もあった。eメールをプリントアウトしたのもあった。毎月、最良のものを5、6本選んで、『すべてを俎上に』で放送できるよう20分にまとめた。それは実にやり甲斐のある作業だった。これまで取り組んだなかで、こんなに刺激を受けた仕事もそうざらにない。たしかに苦労した時もあった。何度か、とりわけ投稿が多かった時期には、一気に60か70の物語を読む破目になった。そんなときは、コテンパンに叩きのめされたよう

from the chair feeling ❶pulverized, absolutely ❷drained of energy. So many emotions to ❸contend with, so many strangers camped out in the living room, so many voices coming at me from so many different directions. On those evenings, for the space of two or three hours, I have felt that the entire population of America has walked into my house. ❹I didn't hear America singing. I heard it telling stories.

🎧 006

Yes, a number of ❺rants and diatribes have been sent in by ❻deranged people, but far fewer than I would have predicted. I have been exposed to ❼groundbreaking ❽revelations about the Kennedy assassination, subjected to several complex ❾exegeses that link current events to ❿verses from Scripture, and ⓫made privy to information ⓬pertaining to lawsuits against half a dozen corporations and government agencies. Some people have gone out of their way to provoke me and turn my stomach. Just last week, I received a submission from a man who signed his story "⓭Cerberus" and gave his return address as "The Underworld 66666." In the story, he told about his days in Vietnam as a ⓮marine, ending with an account of how he and the other men in his company had roasted a stolen Vietnamese baby and eaten it around a campfire. He made it sound as though he were proud of what he had done. ⓯For all I know, the story could be true. But that doesn't mean I have any interest in presenting it on the radio.

---

❶pulverize: 〜をぶちのめす、めためたに負かす　❷drained of ...: 〜をすっかり奪われて　❸contend with ...: 〜と戦う　❹I didn't hear America singing: 19世紀の詩人ウォルト・ホイットマン (Walt Whitman) の有名な一節 "I hear America singing" をふまえている　❺rants and diatribes: 罵詈雑言　❻deranged: 狂った　❼groundbreaking: 独創的な、革新的な　❽revelation: 意外な事実、暴露　❾exegeses: exegesis ([特に聖書の] 評釈、解釈) の複数形　❿verse from Scripture: 聖書の文章　⓫(be) made privy to ...: (秘密・陰謀など) を明かされる

な、精力もとことん吸い取られた気分で椅子から立ち上がった。私はさまざまな感情を相手に格闘し、リビングルームには何人もの見知らぬ隣人がキャンプを張り、ありとあらゆる方向から無数の声が私めがけて飛んできた。そうした晩には、2時間か3時間のあいだ、アメリカの全人口がわが家に上がり込んできた気分だった。アメリカが歌うのが聞こえる、とホイットマンは言った。私はそうではなかった。アメリカが物語を語るのが私には聞こえたのだ。

たしかに、錯乱した人々から、暴言や罵倒がいくつか送られてきはしたが、それも意外に少なかった。ケネディ暗殺に関するあっと驚く真実も知らされたし、時事問題を聖書の一節と結びつけた込み入った講釈も聞かされたし、半ダースばかりの企業や政府機関の訴訟問題をめぐって内幕を教えられたりもした。中には、わざわざ私を挑発し、私の胃袋をひっくり返そうと企てた人もいた。つい先週にも、「ケルベロス（地獄の番犬）」と名のる、住所を「冥界66666番地」と記した男性からの投稿を受けとった。それは海兵隊員としてベトナムで過ごした日々を語った文章だったが、その結末に、中隊仲間と一緒にベトナム人の赤ん坊をさらって丸焼きにし、キャンプファイアを囲んでみんなで食べたという記述があった。そういう話が、得意げな口調で語られていたのである。作り話だと決めつけるつもりはない。本当にそういうことが起きたのかもしれない。だがだからといって、それをラジオで紹介する気にさせられるかどうかは別である。

⓬ pertaining to . . .: 〜に関する　⓭ Cerberus: ケルベロス（ギリシア神話で冥府を守る頭が3つある犬。地獄の番犬）　⓮ marine: 米国海兵隊員　⓯ for all I know: よくわからないけれども、ひょっとしたら

🎧 007

On the other hand, some of the pieces from ❶disturbed people have contained ❷startling and ❸arresting passages. In the fall of 1999, when the project was just getting underway, one came in from another Vietnam ❹vet, a man serving a ❺life sentence for murder in a ❻penitentiary somewhere in the Midwest. He enclosed a handwritten ❼affidavit that ❽recounted the ❾muddled story of how he came to commit his crime, and the last sentence of the document read: "I have never been perfect, but I am real." In some sense, that statement could stand as the ❿credo of the *National Story Project*, the very ⓫principle behind it. We have never been perfect, but we are real.

🎧 008

Of the five thousand stories I have read, most have been ⓬compelling enough to hold me until the last word. Most have been written with simple, ⓭straightforward ⓮conviction, and most have ⓯done honor to the people who sent them in. We all have inner lives. We all feel that we are part of the world and yet ⓰exiled from it. We all burn with the fires of our own existence. Words are needed to express what is in us, and again and again contributors have thanked me for giving them the chance to tell their stories, for "allowing the people to be heard." What the people have said is often astonishing. More than ever, I have come to ⓱appreciate how deep-

---

❶disturbed:(心に)病を抱えた　❷startling: 驚くべき　❸arresting: 注意［興味］を引く　❹vet: =veteran(退役軍人、復員軍人)　❺life sentence: 終身刑、無期懲役　❻penitentiary:(重罪)刑務所　❼affidavit: 宣誓供述書　❽recount:〜を物語る　❾muddled: 混乱した　❿credo: 信条　⓫principle: 原理、原則　⓬compelling: 人の心をつかんで離さない、読みごたえのある　⓭straightforward: 偽りのない、正直な　⓮conviction: 確信、信念　⓯do honor to ...:〜の名誉となる、恥にならない　⓰exiled: 追放された　⓱appreciate:〜を実感する

その一方で、心を病んだ人々からの投稿を読んでいると、ハッとさせられる印象的な一節も多かった。1999年の秋、プロジェクトがそろそろ軌道に乗りかけていたころ、やはりこれもベトナム復員兵だったのだが、殺人罪で中西部の刑務所で無期懲役刑に服している男性からの投稿が届いた。送られてきた手書きの供述書には、自分がいかなる経緯で犯罪を犯すに至ったかが混乱した文章で綴られ、最後の一文は「私は完璧であったことはありませんが、私は現実なのです」となっていた。ある意味で、この言葉はナショナル・ストーリー・プロジェクトのモットーだと言ってもよいかもしれない。これこそこの本の背後にある根本原理である。私たちは完璧であったことはないが、私たちは現実なのだ。

　私が読んだ5000の物語のうち、そのほとんどは最後の一語まで読みたくなるだけの力を備えていた。ほとんどはシンプルで率直な確信を込めて書かれていて、書き手にとって名誉にこそなれ少しも恥ではない出来だった。私たちにはみな内なる人生がある。我々はみな、自分を世界の一部と感じつつ、世界から追放されていると感じてもいる。一人ひとりがみな、己の生の炎をたぎらせている。そして自分のなかにあるものを伝えるには言葉が要る。何度も何度も、私は投稿者から礼を言われた。物語を語るチャンスを与えてくれてありがとう、「庶民の声をみんなに聞いてもらう」機会を作ってくれてありがとう、と。「庶民」たちはしばしば驚くべき物語を語った。何よりもまず、私たちの大半が、どれ

ly and passionately most of us live within ourselves. Our ❶attachments are ❷ferocious. Our loves overwhelm us, define us, ❸obliterate the boundaries between ourselves and others. Fully a third of the stories I have read are about families: parents and children, children and parents, wives and husbands, brothers and sisters, grandparents. For most of us, those are the people who fill up our world, and in story after story, both the dark ones and the humorous ones, I have been impressed by how clearly and forcefully these connections have been ❹articulated.

🎧009

A few high-school students sent in stories about hitting homeruns and winning medals at ❺track meets, but ❻it was the rare adult who took advantage of the occasion to ❼brag about his accomplishments. ❽Hilarious ❾blunders, ❿wrenching coincidences, ⓫brushes with death, miraculous encounters, ⓬improbable ironies, ⓭premonitions, sorrows, pains, dreams—these were the subjects the contributors chose to write about. I learned that I am not alone in my belief that the more we understand of the world, the more ⓮elusive and ⓯confounding the world becomes. As one early contributor so ⓰eloquently put it: "I am left without an adequate definition of reality." If you aren't certain about things, if your mind is still open enough to question what you are seeing, you tend to look at the world with great care, and out of that ⓱watchfulness comes the possibility of seeing something that no one else has seen before.

---

❶attachment: 愛着　❷ferocious:（感情などが）激しい　❸obliterate: 〜を消し去る　❹articulate:（考えなど）をはっきり言葉にする　❺track meet: 陸上競技会　❻it is the rare . . . who 〜: 〜する…は稀だ　❼brag about . . .: 〜を自慢する　❽hilarious: ひどくおかしい　❾blunder: 大失敗、へま　❿wrenching: 胸を締めつけるような、深刻な　⓫brush: 軽い接触　⓬improbable: ありそうにもない　⓭premonition: 予感、兆候　⓮elusive: とらえ所のない、いわく言いがたい　⓯confounding: 途方に暮れさせるような　⓰eloquently: 雄弁に

ほど深く、情熱的に内なる生を生きているかを私は思い知らされた。我々の抱く愛着はこの上なく激しく、我々の情愛は我々を圧倒し、規定し、我々と他人を区切る境界を消し去る。読んだ物語のうち、家族をめぐるものは3分の1にも及ぶ。親と子、子と親、夫婦、兄弟姉妹、祖父母。私たちの大半にとって、自分の世界を埋めているのはまさにそうした人たちなのだ。暗い話であれ愉快な話であれ、そうした絆が次々あざやかに、力強く言葉にされていることに私は感じ入らずにいられなかった。

　ホームランを打ったとか、陸上競技でメダルを取ったとかいった話を送ってきた高校生も少しはいたが、この機会を自慢話に利用する大人はめったにいなかった。爆笑もののヘマ、胸を締めつけられるような偶然、死とのニアミス、奇跡のような遭遇、およそありえない皮肉、もろもろの予兆、悲しみ、痛み、夢。投稿者たちが取り上げたのはそういったテーマだった。世界について知れば知るほど、世界はますます捉えがたい、ますます混乱させられる場になっていくと信じているのは自分一人ではないことを私は知った。いち早く投稿してくれたある人がいみじくも言ったように、「私はもう現実をうまく定義できない」。物事について考えを固めてしまわず、見えているものを疑うよう心を開いておけば、世界を眺める目も丁寧になる。そうした注意深さから、いままで誰も見たことのない何かが見えてくる可能性も出てくる。自分が何もかも

❶ watchfulness: 油断のないこと

You have to be willing to admit that you don't have all the answers. If you think you do, you will never have anything important to say.

🎧010

Incredible ❶plots, unlikely ❷turns, events that refuse to obey the laws of common sense. ❸More often than not, our lives resemble the stuff of ❹eighteenth-century novels. Just today, another ❺batch of e-mails from NPR arrived at my door, and among the new submissions was this story from a woman who lives in San Diego, California. I quote from it not because it is unusual, but simply because it is the freshest piece of evidence at hand:

🎧011

I was ❻adopted from an ❼orphanage at the age of eight months. Less than a year later, my adoptive father died suddenly. I was raised by my ❽widowed mother with three older adopted brothers. When you are adopted, there is a natural curiosity to know your birth family. By the time I was married and in my late twenties, I decided to start looking.

🎧012

I had been raised in ❾Iowa, and sure enough, after a two-year search, I ❿located my ⓫birth mother in ⓬Des Moines. We met and went to dinner. I asked her who my birth father was, and she gave me his name. I asked where he lived, and she said "San Diego," which was where I had been living for the last five years. I had moved to San Diego not knowing a ⓭soul—just knowing I wanted to be there.

---

❶plot:（小説などの）筋、構想　❷turn:（状況などの）変化、展開　❸more often than not: しばしば　❹eighteenth-century novels: 18世紀の小説は19〜21世紀の小説に較べ途方もない偶然に頼ることが多い　❺batch: 束　❻adopt: 〜を養子にする　❼orphanage: 孤児院　❽widowed: 未亡人の　❾Iowa: アイオワ（米国中部の州）　❿locate: 〜の所在を突き止める　⓫birth mother: 実母　⓬Des Moines: デモイン（アイオワ州中南部、州都）　⓭soul:（否定文で）1人も〜ない、誰も〜ない

答えを持っているわけではないと認めることが肝要なのだ。すべて答えを持っていると思っている人には、大切なことは何ひとつ言えないだろう。

　信じがたい展開、ありえない成り行き、常識の法則をまるで無視した出来事。我々の人生はしばしば18世紀小説の素材のように思える。つい今日も、NPRからさらなるeメールの束がわが家に届いたが、それら最新の投稿のなかに、カリフォルニア州サンディエゴに住む女性が送ってきたこんな物語があった。ここでこれを引用するのは、これがべつに例外的だからではなく、あくまで手元にある最新の実例だからである。

　私は生後8カ月で孤児院から引きとられて養子になりました。それから1年と経たないうちに、養父が突然亡くなりました。未亡人となった養母は、やはり養子だったほか3人の子供とともに私を育ててくれました。養子になった人間は、自分の実の親に好奇心を抱くものです。20代後半になって、すでに結婚もしていた私は、探してみることにしました。

　私はアイオワで育てられたのですが、果たせるかな、2年探した末に、実の母親がアイオワ州デモインにいることがわかりました。会いにいって、二人で食事に出かけました。実の父親は誰なのかと訊いてみると、名前を教えてくれました。どこに住んでいるのかと訊くと、「サンディエゴ」という答えが返ってきました。サンディエゴは私が5年前から住んでいる街です。サンディエゴに移ったとき、知りあいは一人もいませんでした。とにかくサンディエゴで暮らしたいという気持ちがあるだけでした。

🎧013

It ended up that I worked in the building next door to where my father worked. We often ate lunch at the same restaurant. We never told his wife of my existence, as I didn't really want to ❶disrupt his life. He had always been a bit of a ❷gadabout, however, and he always had a girlfriend ❸on the side. He and his last girlfriend were "together" for fifteen-plus years, and she remained the source of my information about him.

🎧014

Five years ago, my birth mother was dying of cancer in Iowa. Simultaneously, I received a call from my father's ❹paramour that he had died of heart ❺complications. I called my ❻biological mother in the hospital in Iowa and told her of his death. She died that night. I received ❼word that both of their funerals were held on the following Saturday at exactly the same hour—his at 11 a.m. in California and hers at 1 p.m. in Iowa.

🎧015

After three or four months, I sensed that a book was going to be necessary to ❽do justice to the project. Too many good stories were coming in, and it wasn't possible for me to present more than a ❾fraction of the worthy submissions on the radio. Many of them were too long for the format we had established, and the ❿ephemeral nature of the broadcasts (a ⓫lone, ⓬disembodied voice floating

---

❶disrupt: 〜をかき乱す　❷gadabout: 遊び人、遊び歩く人　❸on the side: おまけに、ひそかに　❹paramour: 愛人、恋人　❺complication: 合併症、併発症　❻biological: 生物学上の、血のつながった　❼word: 便り、知らせ　❽do justice to . . .: 〜を正当に扱う　❾fraction:（全体の）一部分　❿ephemeral: はかない、短命の　⓫lone: 孤立した、独りきりの　⓬disembodied: 肉体を持たない、実体のない

あれこれ調べた結果、私の勤め先があるビルは、父の勤め先の隣にあることが判明しました。私たちはよく同じレストランで昼ご飯を食べていたのです。父の生活をかき乱す気は毛頭なかったので、父のいまの奥さんに私の存在を知らせたりはしませんでした。もっとも父は、昔からちょっとした遊び人だったらしく、いつも内緒のガールフレンドがいたようです。最後のガールフレンドは15年以上「一緒」だった人で、私にとってもずっと、父に関する情報源となってくれました。

　5年前、アイオワにいる実の母が癌で死にかけていました。それと同時に、父の恋人から電話があって、父が心臓の合併症で亡くなったと知らされました。私はアイオワの母の入院先に電話して、父の死を伝えました。母はその晩に亡くなりました。二人の葬儀が、来る土曜のまったく同じ時間に行なわれることを私は知らされました —— 父の葬儀はカリフォルニアで午前11時から、母の葬儀はアイオワで午後1時から。

　3、4カ月続けたあたりで、プロジェクトの可能性を十分活かすには本が必要だという気がしてきた。よい話があまりにたくさん届くので、放送に値する物語のうちごく一部しか紹介できないのだ。放送用に定めたフォーマットには長すぎるものも多かったし、ラジオという媒介のはかなさを思うと（肉体から切り離されたただ一人の声が、毎月20分足らず、放送波に

across the American ❶airwaves for eighteen or twenty minutes every month) made me want to collect the most memorable ones and preserve them in written form. Radio is a powerful tool, and NPR reaches into almost every corner of the country, but you can't hold the words in your hands. A book is ❷tangible, and once you put it down, you can return to the place where you left it and pick it up again.

🎧016

This ❸anthology contains what I consider to be the best of the approximately five thousand works that have come in during the past two years. But it is also a representative selection, a ❹miniaturized version of the *National Story Project* as a whole. For every story about a dream or an animal or a missing object to be found here, there were dozens of others that were submitted, dozens of others that could have been chosen. The selection begins with a six-sentence tale about a chicken (the first story I read on the air in November in 1999) and ends with a ❺wistful ❻meditation on the role that radio plays in our lives. The author of that last piece, Ameni Rozsa, was moved to write her story while listening to one of the *National Story Project* broadcasts. I had been hoping to capture bits and fragments of American reality, but it had never occurred to me that the project itself could become a part of that reality, too.

🎧017

This book has been written by people of all ages and ❼from all

---

❶airwave: 電波　❷tangible: (物体などが)触れることができる　❸anthology: (いろいろな人の作品を集めた)作品集　❹miniaturized: ミニチュアの　❺wistful: 切ない、哀切な　❻meditation: 考察、省察　❼from all walks of life: あらゆる階層の

乗ってアメリカを漂うだけ)、やはり、とりわけ記憶に残る話を集めて文字の形で保存したかった。ラジオは強力な道具であり、NPRならほぼ全米に届くわけだが、それでも、ラジオの言葉を両手に持つことはできない。本なら手で触れることができるし、読むのをやめても、いずれまたそれを置いたところに戻って手にとれる。

　このアンソロジーには、この2年間に送られてきたおよそ5000点のうち、私から見て最良の物語が収められている。と同時にこれは、いわばナショナル・ストーリー・プロジェクト全体のミニチュア版というか、全体の傾向を伝えるような選択にもなっている。この本に収められることになった、夢、動物、なくした物等々に関する物語一つひとつに対し、代わりに選ばれてもよかった同テーマの物語がそれぞれ何ダースかずつあったのだ。この本は一羽の鶏をめぐる6センテンスの話ではじまり(これは1999年の11月、放送で一番最初に朗読した話である)、ラジオが私たちの人生で果たす役割をめぐる哀切な考察で終わる。最後の話を書いたアメニ・ローザは、まさにラジオでナショナル・ストーリー・プロジェクトの放送を聞いている最中に自分も書こうと思い立ったのだ。アメリカの現実のかけらや断片をつかまえたいとは私も願っていたが、まさかプロジェクト自体がその現実の一部になるとは思わなかった。

　この本はあらゆる階層に属する、あらゆる年齢の人々によって書かれ

walks of life. Among them are a postman, a ❶merchant seaman, a trolley-bus driver, a gas-and-electric-meter reader, a ❷restorer of ❸player pianos, a crime-scene cleaner, a musician, a businessman, two priests, an ❹inmate at a state ❺correctional facility, several doctors, and ❻assorted housewives, farmers, and ❼ex-servicemen. The youngest contributor is barely twenty; the oldest is pushing ninety. Half of the writers are women; half are men. They live in cities, suburbs, and in rural areas, and they come from forty-two different states. In making my choices, I never once gave a thought to ❽demographic balance. I selected the stories solely on the basis of ❾merit: for their humanity, for their truth, for their charm. The numbers just fell out that way, and the results were determined by blind chance.

🎧018

In an attempt to make some order out of this chaos of voices and contrasting styles, I have broken the stories into ten different categories. The section titles ❿speak for themselves, but except for the fourth section, "⓫Slapstick," which is made up entirely of comic stories, there is a wide range of material within each of the categories. Their contents ⓬run the gamut from ⓭farce to tragic drama, and for every act of cruelty and violence that one encounters in them, there is a ⓮countervailing act of kindness or generosity or love. The stories go back and forth, up and down, in and out, and after a while your head starts to spin. Turn the page from one con-

---

❶merchant seaman: 商船船員　❷restorer: 修復人　❸player piano: 自動ピアノ　❹inmate:（施設・刑務所などの）被収容者　❺correctional facility: 矯正施設、刑務所　❻assorted: さまざまな　❼ex-serviceman: 退役軍人　❽demographic: 人口分布上の　❾merit: 価値　❿speak for themselves: 説明を要しない　⓫slapstick: スラップスティック、どたばた喜劇　⓬run the gamut: 全域にわたる　⓭farce: ファルス、茶番劇　⓮countervail: 〜を相殺する

た。書き手には郵便局員もいれば商船員もいるし、トロリーバスの運転手、ガスと電気のメーター検針員、自動ピアノの修復職人、犯行現場清掃業者、ミュージシャン、会社経営者、司祭(二人)、州立懲正施設の住人、医師数名、そして主婦や農場経営者や元軍人が大勢いる。最年少の寄稿者はようやく20歳に達したところであり、最年長は90にならんとしている。書き手の半数は女性、半数は男性。都市、郊外、田舎と住む場所もまちまちであり、州の数で見ると42州。物語を選ぶにあたって、地理的なバランスはいっさい考慮しなかった。選んだ基準はあくまで物語自体であり、その人間らしさ、真実性、その魅力である。そのような分布はひとりでに生じたのであって、あくまで偶然の産物である。

　多種多様な声や対照的なスタイルから成るこの混沌に、ある種の秩序を与えるため、物語は10のカテゴリーに分類してある。各セクションのタイトルの意味は自明だと思うが、もっぱらコミカルな物語から成る第4セクション「スラップスティック」を例外として、どのセクションもさまざまに異なるトーンの物語が一緒になっている。内容は笑劇(ファルス)から悲劇まであらゆる領域にわたり、そのなかで出会う残酷で暴力的な行為一つひとつに対し、それを相殺するかのように、親切な行為、寛大さや愛情に支えられた営みがかならずひとつは出てくる。物語は前に進みうしろに下がり、上へ下へと昇り降りし、出たり入ったりをくり返し、読む方はいつしか頭がくらくらしてくる。ページをめくって寄稿者が変われ

tributor to the next, and you are confronted by an entirely different person, an entirely different set of circumstances, an entirely different worldview. But difference is what this book is all about. There is some elegant and sophisticated writing in it, but there is also much that is ❶crude and ❷awkward. Only a small portion of it resembles anything that could ❸qualify as "literature." It is something else, something raw and close to the bone, and whatever skills these authors might lack, most of their stories are unforgettable. It is difficult for me to imagine that anyone could read through this book from beginning to end without once ❹shedding a tear, without once laughing ❺out loud.

🎧019

If I had to define what these stories were, I would call them ❻dispatches, reports from the front lines of personal experience. They are about the private worlds of individual Americans. Yet again and again one sees the inescapable marks of history on them, the ❼intricate ways in which individual destinies are shaped by society at large. Some of the older contributors, looking back on events from their childhood and youth, are necessarily writing about ❽the Depression and World War II. Other contributors, born in the middle of the century, continue to be ❾haunted by the effects of ❿the war in Vietnam. That conflict ended twenty-five years ago, and yet it lives on in us as a ⓫recurrent nightmare, a great wound in the national soul. Still other contributors, from several different genera-

---

❶crude: 粗雑な　❷awkward: 不器用な、ぎこちない　❸qualify as ...: 〜として通用する　❹shed: (涙・血など)を流す　❺out loud: 大声で　❻dispatch: 緊急の文書(海外特派員からの特電などをいう)　❼intricate: 入り組んだ　❽the Depression: 世界大恐慌(1929年10月のニューヨーク市場の大暴落を契機に発生した世界的な大不況)　❾haunted: (妙な考え・思い出などに)とり憑かれた　❿the war in Vietnam: ベトナム戦争(1954_75)　⓫recurrent: くり返し起きている

ば、また全然違う人間とあなたは向き合い、全然別の環境、全然別の世界観に出会う。だがそうした違いこそこの本の真髄である。優雅で洗練された文章もいくつかあるが、荒削りでぎこちないものもたくさんある。「文学」という名に少しでも適合しそうなものはごくわずかである。これは文学とは違う何かなのだ。もっと生な、もっと骨に近いところにある何かなのであって、いわゆる文章術には欠けるものも多くとも、ほとんどすべての物語に忘れがたい力がみなぎっている。誰かがこの本を最初から最後まで読んで、一度も涙を流さず一度も声を上げて笑わないという事態は想像しがたい。

　これらの物語をあえて定義するなら、「至急報(ディスパッチ)」と呼びたい。つまり、個人個人の体験の前線から送られてきた報告。アメリカ人一人ひとりのプライベートな世界に関する物語でありながら、そこに逃れがたい歴史の爪あとが残っているのを読み手はくり返し目にすることになる。個人の運命が、社会全体によってかたちづくられていくその入り組んださまを再三再四思い知らされるのだ。年輩の寄稿者が幼いころ、若いころをふり返るなら、おのずとそれは、大恐慌や第二次大戦について書くことになる。20世紀なかばに生まれた寄稿者たちはベトナム戦争の影響にいまだとり憑かれている。25年前に終わった戦いだというのに、それはいまも我々のうちに、くり返し訪れる悪夢として、国民全体の胸のうちに残る大きな傷として生きつづけている。また、アメリカの人種差別

tions, have written stories about the disease of American racism. This ❶scourge has been with us for more than three hundred-fifty years, and no matter how hard we struggle to ❷eradicate it from our midst, a cure has yet to be found.

🎧020

Other stories touch on AIDS, alcoholism, drug abuse, pornography and guns. Social forces are forever ❸impinging on the lives of these people, but not one of their stories sets out to document society ❹per se. We know that Janet Zupan's father died in a prison camp in Vietnam in 1967, but that is not what her story is about. With a remarkable eye for visual detail, she tracks a single afternoon in ❺the Mojave Desert as her father chases after his stubborn and ❻recalcitrant horse, and knowing what we do about what will happen to her father just two years later, we read her account as a kind of memorial to him. Not a word about the war, and yet by indirection and an almost ❼painterly focus on the moment before her, we sense that an entire era of American history is passing in front of our eyes.

🎧021

Stan Benkoski's father's laugh. The ❽slap to Carol Sherman Jones's face. Little Mary Grace Dembeck dragging a Christmas tree through the streets of Brooklyn. John Keith's mother's missing wedding ring. John Flannelly's fingers stuck in the holes of a stainless steel heating ❾grate. Mel Singer wrestled to the floor by

---

❶scourge: 災い ❷eradicate: 〜を根絶する、撲滅する ❸impinge on . . .: 〜に影響を与える、(自由・権利)を侵害する ❹per se: それ自体 ❺the Mojave Desert: モハーヴィ砂漠(カリフォルニア州南部の砂漠) ❻recalcitrant: 手に負えない、扱いにくい ❼painterly: 画家のような ❽slap: 平手打ち ❾grate: (暖炉の)火格子

の病をめぐる物語を書いた寄稿者はあらゆる世代に広がっている。3世紀半以上にわたって我々とともにあるこの災いは、我々の懸命の努力にもかかわらず、いまだ解決策が見つかっていないのだ。

　エイズ、アルコール依存症、ドラッグ中毒、ポルノグラフィ、銃に触れた話もある。社会からの圧力はこの本に出てくる人々の生活をつねに圧迫しているが、社会そのものを記録しようとしている物語はひとつもない。ジャネット・ズーパンの父親が1967年にベトナムの捕虜収容所で死んだことを私たちは知るが、それが彼女の話のテーマではない。視覚的なディテールを実に見事に捉える目でもって、モハーヴィ砂漠でのある日の午後、父親がわがままで強情な馬を追いかける姿を彼女は追ってみせる。そして、ほんの2年後に父親の身に何が起きるかを知る我々は、それを父に対して捧げられた一種のメモリアルとして読む。戦争には一言も触れていないのに、間接的に、眼前の瞬間をほとんど絵を描くかのように焦点が絞られていることによって、アメリカの歴史におけるひとつの時代がまるごと自分の目の前を過ぎていくのを我々は感じるのだ。

　スタン・ベンコスキーの父親の笑い声。キャロル・シャーマン＝ジョーンズの顔に浴びせられた平手打ち。クリスマスツリーを引きずってブルックリンの街を歩く幼いメアリ・グレース・デンベック。ジョン・キースの母親のなくなった結婚指輪。ステンレスの火格子の穴にはまったジョン・フラネリーの指。自分のコートにねじ伏せられて床に倒

his own coat. Anna Thorson at the ❶barn dance. Edith Riemer's bicycle. Marie Johnson watching a movie shot in the house where she lived as a girl. Ludlow Perry's encounter with the legless man. Catherine Austin Alexander looking out her window on West Seventy-fourth Street. Juliana C. Nash's walk through the snow. Dede Ryan's philosophical martini. Carolyn Brasher's regrets. Mary McCallum's father's dream. Earl Roberts's collar button. One by one, these stories leave a lasting impression on the mind. Even after you have read through all of them, they continue to stay with you, and you find yourself remembering them in the same way that you remember a ❷trenchant parable or a good joke. The images are clear, ❸dense, and yet somehow weightless. And each one is small enough to fit inside your pocket. Like the snapshots we carry around of our own families.

Paul Auster
October 3, 2000

---

❶ barn dance: バーンダンス（米国で生まれた社交ダンスの一種。元々は納屋で催された陽気な集い）
❷ trenchant: 辛らつな、鋭い　❸ dense: 濃密な

れているメル・シンガー。バーンダンスでのアンナ・ソーソン。イーディス・ライマーの自転車。幼いころ自分が住んでいた家で撮影された映画を観るマリー・ジョンソン。ラドロー・ペリーと脚のない男との出会い。部屋の窓から西74丁目を眺めるキャサリン・オースティン・アレグザンダー。雪の街を歩くジュリアナ・C・ナッシュ。ディーディ・ライアンの哲学的マティーニ。キャロリン・ブラッシャーの後悔。メアリ・マッカラムの父が見た夢。アール・ロバーツの襟のボタン。一つひとつ、忘れがたい印象をこれらの物語は残す。物語がたくさん積み重なっていっても、なおも心に残り、中味の濃い寓話やよくできたジョークが記憶に残るのと同じように、ふっと頭に浮かんでくる。イメージは明確で、濃密で、にもかかわらずなぜか軽々としている。一つひとつの物語がポケットに入るくらい小さいのだ。ちょうど私たちが持ち歩く、家族のスナップ写真のように。

ポール・オースター
2000年10月3日

編訳者まえがき

『ポール・オースターが朗読する
ナショナル・ストーリー・プロジェクト』の楽しみ方

> *I hear America singing, the varied carols I hear,*
> *Those of mechanics, each one singing his as it should be blithe and strong,*
> *The carpenter singing his as he measures his plank or beam,*
> *The mason singing his as he makes ready for work, or leaves off work,*
> *The boatman singing what belongs to him in his boat, the deckhand singing on the steamboat deck …*
> (アメリカがうたうのがきこえる、いろんなよろこびのうたがきこえる、
> 職人たちがそれぞれ、職人らしく　明るくたくましくうたっている、
> 大工は板や梁の寸法を測りながら　じぶんのうたをうたい、
> 石工は仕事の支度をしながら、後片付けをしながらうたい、
> 船頭は船に乗り　じぶんとつながったものたちをうたい、甲板員は蒸気船の甲板でうたい……）

——ウォルト・ホイットマンがこううたったのが、南北戦争が勃発する直前の1860年。その後もさまざまな形で、人々の「うた」や「声」にアメリカは耳を傾けてきた。社会学者リンド夫妻による、綿密な聞き取り調査に基づいてアメリカの平均的な町の平均的な人々の暮らしを綴った『ミドルタウン』(1929; 邦訳青木書店)。『仕事！』(1974; 邦訳晶文社)、『アメリカン・ドリーム』(1980; 邦訳白水社)をはじめとする、スタッズ・ター

ケルによる一連のインタビュー集。

 とはいえ、この〈ナショナル・ストーリー・プロジェクト〉のように、人々がみずから、「実話であること」を唯一の縛りに内容もスタイルも自由に自分の物語を語り、それがラジオを通して全国規模で聴かれるという事態は、いままでそうめったにはなかったのではないか。編者オースターがイントロダクションでも触れている、「いろんな人にそれぞれ自分の物語を書いてもらえばいいのよ」というシリ・ハストヴェットの思いつきは、ひょっとするとアメリカの文化に対するものすごく大きな貢献かもしれない。

 この本の元になっている、*I Thought My Father Was God: And Other True Tales from NPR's National Story Project*（2001; Picador USA, 2002／邦訳『ナショナル・ストーリー・プロジェクト』新潮社）がどのように生まれたかは、本書にも収めたイントロダクションでオースターが詳しく述べているので、そちらをご覧いただければと思う。オースターが、エッセイ集『トゥルー・ストーリーズ』（新潮社）でも「実話」を数多く題材に取り上げ、インタビュー（アルク刊『ナイン・インタビューズ　柴田元幸と9人の作家たち』など）や小説でも「実話」に惹かれていることをくり返し表明してきたことを思えば、彼がいずれこのような仕事に手を染めるのは、もしかしたら必然だったのかもしれない。いずれにせよ、実話への興味、朗読上手、熱意、オースターがあわせ持つそうした要素があいまって、すばらしい物語集が出来上がった。ほかの誰がやっても、これほどの質と量が達成できたとは思えない。

『ナショナル・ストーリー・プロジェクト』には179本の物語が収められているが、このうち130本を選んでオースターが朗読したテープが、Harper Audio からカセット6本組みで発売されている。このCDブックは、これら130本のなかからさらに厳選して18本を選び、オースターのイントロを加え、左に原文、右に新潮社版『ナショナル・ストーリー・プロジェクト』に基づく訳文を配して、音声付き対訳版にしたものである。まさに文字どおり「アメリカが語るのが聞こえる」本と言ってよいと思う。幸いにして本書が好評を博したら、残り112本についても続篇を出したいと思っている。

　この本をどのように読むか／聞くかについては、むろん読者一人ひとりが決めてくだされればよいことだが、一言だけお節介を言うと、日本語を読むことからはじめるのはいかにももったいない。耳からであれ目からであれ、まずはナマの声に触れるところからはじめていただければと思う。

　対訳CD本を作る上での煩雑な作業を一手に引き受けてくださったのは、『ナイン・インタビューズ』でもお世話になったアルクの白川雅敏さんである。白川さんの熱意のおかげで、聴いて楽しく読んで楽しい、かつモノとしても美しい本が出来上がった。この場をお借りして深く感謝する。

柴田元幸
2005年7月

新装版のための編訳者まえがき

　アメリカの名もない個人たちが自分の生涯の物語を語り、それらの物語に心を打たれた作家ポール・オースターが物語集を編纂する。こうして出来上がった『ナショナル・ストーリー・プロジェクト』のなかから厳選して、英日対訳とオースターによる朗読を組みあわせて作ったこの本が最初に出たのは2005年。もう15年近く前ということになる。今日の出版状況にあっては、15年という時間は、たいていの本にとって忘却の彼方に消えてしまうのに十分な長さだろうと思う。そのなかでこの本が、読者の要望に応えていままた復活することになって、訳者代表としてはとても嬉しい。

　2001年に『ナショナル・ストーリー・プロジェクト』を刊行して以来、ポール・オースターは長篇小説8冊、回想録2冊を発表している。『NSP』の前と後とではまったく作風が違う、などとはもちろん言えないが、強いて言うなら、『NSP』以降には、一冊の長篇が複数の人物の物語から成っている度合いが、以前よりだいぶ大きいということは言える気がする。特に最近では、『サンセット・パーク』(2010、邦訳は2020年刊行予定)において章ごとに違う視点的人物を導入し、900ページ近い最新作『４３２１』(2017、未訳) では逆に一人の人物が章ごとに違う生を生きるといった形にまで展開している。もちろんそれ以前の小説も、決して一人だけの人間の姿しか見えてこない小説ではなかったが、群像劇的な要素はやはりかなり増していて、それが一連の近作に、以前の作品とは違う種類の奥行きを与えているように思う。

　いまこの本をあらためて見てみると、個々の物語の魅力もさることな

がら、編者オースターに目を向けてみるなら、物語作者が自分の物語を語る義務から一時的に解放されて、他人の物語にひたすら耳を傾け、それらに魅了されている姿が見えてくる。そしてそのオースターによる朗読に、今度は我々読者が耳を傾け、魅了される。そういう幸福の波及がこの本にはあったんだな、と呑気な訳者はいまごろになって認識している。その波及がもう一度生じるのだと思うと、本当に嬉しい。より多くの皆さんに楽しんでいただけますように。

柴田元幸

2019年11月

🎧 022-037

ANIMALS

動物

🎧 023

THE CHICKEN

　As I was walking down Stanton Street early one Sunday morning, I saw a chicken a few yards ahead of me. I was walking faster than the chicken, so I gradually caught up. By the time we approached Eighteenth Avenue, I was close behind. The chicken turned south on Eighteenth. At the fourth house along, it turned in at the walk, hopped up the front steps, and rapped sharply on the metal ❶storm door with its ❷beak. After a moment, the door opened and the chicken went in.

Linda Elegant
Portland, Oregon

※トラック022をはじめ、オースターによる導入のナレーションのスクリプトは、232〜235ページにまとめて掲載されています。
❶storm door: 防風ドア（入り口のドアの外側に取り付ける）　❷beak:（鳥の）くちばし

鶏

　ある日曜の朝早くにスタントン通りを歩いていると、何メートルか先に一羽の鶏が見えた。私の方が歩みが速かったので、じきに追いついていった。十八番街も近くなってきたころには、鶏のすぐうしろまで来ていた。十八番街で、鶏は南に曲がった。角から4軒目の家まで来ると、私道に入っていき、玄関前の階段をぴょんぴょん上がって、金属の防風ドアをくちばしで鋭く叩いた。やや間があって、ドアが開き、鶏は中に入っていった。

リンダ・エレガント
オレゴン州ポートランド

🎧 025

VERTIGO

When I was ten, my family moved to Apple Valley, a small community in the California High Desert. My father was a test pilot who had been ❶stationed at George Air Force Base since the summer of 1964. We settled in a mustard-colored house situated in a vast neighborhood that included a couple of other houses, a thousand ❷creosote bushes, ❸Joshua trees, and ❹pear cacti on a three-mile stretch in every direction but one: the Mojave River blinked at us a mile down desert.

🎧 026

My father was six-three and had incredible, bushy eyebrows. He had a laugh so deep I could feel its ❺peals vibrate in my own stomach. He could imitate a horse's ❻whinny like no one I've ever met. He spoke a Taiwanese dialect and enough German to seem fluent. He used to give one-man air shows in the communities where he lived, and his picture hung in a gas station in his hometown, where he was considered a local hero. He died in a prison camp in North Vietnam in 1967, when he was forty-one.

🎧 027

I realize that I cherished my father for his strengths. He had a spirited investment in taking chances and a bottomless reservoir of optimism. When we lived in Taiwan, he rode the bus every week

---

（タイトル）Vertigo: ここでは馬の名前だが、本来は「めまい」の意　❶station: 〜を配属する　❷creosote bush: メキシコハマビシ（ハマビシ科の常緑低木）　❸Joshua tree: ヨシュアノキ（米国西部の砂漠地帯に生える常緑樹ユッカの一種）　❹pear cacti: ナシサボテン（単数形はpear cactus）　❺peal: （笑い声などの）響き　❻whinny: （馬の）いななき

ヴァーティゴ

　私が10歳のとき、うちはアップルヴァレーに引越した。アップルヴァレーはカリフォルニア・ハイデザート地域にある小さな村である。私の父はテストパイロットで、1964年の夏以来ジョージ空軍基地に配属されていた。だだっ広い村に建つ、芥子色(からし)の家に私たちは落ち着いた。周りにはほかに何軒かよその家が散在するだけで、その外側には無数のハマビシ、ヨシュアノキ、ナシサボテンが三方にそれぞれ5キロばかり広がっていた。あと一方にはモハーヴィ川が、1キロちょっとの砂漠をはさんだ向こうできらきら光っていた。

　私の父は身の丈190センチ、おそろしく濃い眉をしていた。笑い声はものすごく太くて、その響きが私のお腹まで震わせているのが感じられた。あんなに馬のいななきの真似が上手い人を私はほかに知らない。台湾語の一方言も話せたし、ドイツ語もいちおう流暢(りゅうちょう)に聞こえるくらい喋れた。近隣の人たちを観衆によく一人で航空ショーもやってみせたし、故郷に帰れば英雄扱いでガソリンスタンドに写真が飾ってあった。1967年、北ベトナムの捕虜収容所で父は死んだ。41歳だった。

　あのころの私は、父の強さに何より惹かれていたのだと思う。冒険に挑むということに父は入れ込んでいた。父は底なしの楽天家だった。一家で台湾に住んでいたころは、毎週バスに乗って台北まで出かけていっ

into Taipei, where he and a local carpenter built a ❶Lightning sailboat. We ❷hauled it back to the United States and came in last in every boat race we entered in ❸Chesapeake Bay. My father was always eager to try new things, to bring fun changes to our lives. Sometimes one or the other of us was reluctant or afraid, but he had a way of encouraging us to take a chance.

🎧028

Now that I look back on my father, under the focus of forty-four-year old eyes, I know that what I loved most about him was his ❹fragility, and because I sensed this, I developed a desire to protect him. I think everyone in my family felt the same. We were ❺in awe of his ❻exuberance but ❼cradled fear for him, too. Maybe he carried so much sense of promise that we realized how hard it would be on all of us to see him disappointed, disillusioned, or hurt.

🎧029

Soon after moving to Apple Valley, we adopted a horse we named Vertigo. Vertigo was a big, smart, stubborn ❽palomino, an ex-parade horse whose years of showing off had left him ❾savvy and ❿embittered. I can't speak for my ⓫siblings, but I was afraid of Vertigo. He had a way of knowing my fear, too, and seemed to relish my uneasiness and hesitations, lifting a threatening ⓬hoof or slapping me with his tail whenever I came near. My father, on the other hand, was ready to ride, and spent hours learning the ⓭tack and the

---

❶Lightning: ライトニング級（レース用セールボートの階級の１つ）　❷haul: 〜を輸送する　❸Chesapeake Bay: チェサピーク湾（メリーランド州とヴァージニア州に大西洋が入り込んだ湾）　❹fragility: 壊れやすさ、もろさ　❺in awe of . . .: 〜に畏れの念を抱いて　❻exuberance: あふれんばかりの活力　❼cradle: 〜を抱く、育む　❽palomino: パロミノ（米国南西部で改良された黄金色の毛の馬）　❾savvy: 世慣れた、経験豊富な　❿embittered: 苦々しい思いを抱いた　⓫sibling: （男女の別なく）きょうだい　⓬hoof: ひづめ　⓭tack: 馬具

て、地元の大工と二人で、ライトニング級ヨットを組み立てた。ヨットはアメリカまで持ち帰って、チェサピーク湾で開かれるレースに片っ端から参加してつねに最下位だった。父はいつも新しいことに挑戦していた。私たちの生活に楽しい変化をもたらそうとやる気満々だった。家族の誰かが尻込みしたり、怖がったりしても、うまく励まして、思いきってチャレンジするよう仕向けるのだった。

　44歳になった目で、いま父のことをふり返ってみると、自分が何より愛したのが、父の・も・ろ・さだったことが私にはわかる。そのもろさを感じとったがゆえに、父を護ってあげたいという思いが私の胸のうちに育まれていった。家族はみんな同じ気持ちだったと思う。父の元気一杯ぶりに圧倒されながらも、その身を危ぶむ思いもあったのだ。あんなに多くを約束し期待しているようにふるまっている父が、がっかりしたり、幻滅したり、傷ついたりするのを見るのはどんなにつらいことか。私たちはそれに気づいていたのだと思う。

　アップルヴァレーに移ってまもなく、わが家は馬を一頭もらい受けて、ヴァーティゴと名づけた。頭の切れる、強情な、大きな黄金色の馬で、かつてはパレードに出ていて何年もそのきらびやかな身体を見せびらかしてきたせいで、いまは小賢しい、底意地の悪い性格になっていた。兄や姉については何とも言えないが、私はヴァーティゴが怖かった。しかも相手は、私が怖がっているのをちゃんと見抜いていて、こっちがびくびくためらっているのを楽しんでいる様子だった。私がそばに来るたびに、ひづめを持ち上げて脅かしたり、尻尾でぴしゃっと叩いたりするのだ。一方父は、ヴァーティゴを乗りこなそうと意気込んで、何時

ways of horse care.

🎧030

One Saturday afternoon in July 1965, my father ❶saddled up Vertigo and set out for the Mojave River. We all came down to the ❷corral to watch. Even my mother stayed close by, weeding the ❸ice plant that crawled around the shade of the house. First, my father curried Vertigo's ❹mane and tail; as he worked, the horse reached around and casually ❺lipped the hoof-pick from the corral post; it dropped in the dry dirt. ❻Undaunted, my father checked Vertigo's hooves. Vertigo sighed and ❼snorted and then proceeded to untie the ❽halter rope from the rail. Seconds later, he ❾pranced away. "Rrrrrrmmmph," my father whinnied softly to Vertigo as he reached for the swinging halter rope. He retied the horse to the post and set to work ❿hitching the ⓫bridle, lifting the saddle on, and securing the buckles and ⓬cinch. Vertigo snorted and shook. He nodded his head and slapped my father's face with his mane. "Rrrrrrmmmph," was all my father had to say. Finally, they were ready. The day was hot and dry. It must have been about three in the afternoon.

🎧031

I remember the vision of them heading out—my father shirtless and in jeans and tennis shoes, the horse ⓭plodding along with his head to the ground, starting to ⓮nibble at grass weeds and snorting at ants. My father pulled steadily at the ⓯reins and Vertigo ⓰jerked

---

❶saddle up . . .: 〜に鞍をつける　❷corral: (馬などを入れる)囲い　❸ice plant: アイスプラント(マツバギク属の草)　❹mane: たてがみ　❺lip: 〜に唇を触れる　❻undaunted: ひるまずに　❼snort: 鼻を鳴らす　❽halter: 端綱(馬の頭につけて引く)　❾prance: (馬などが)跳ねながら進む　❿hitch: (かぎ・縄など)をひっかける、巻きつける　⓫bridle: 馬勒(頭部の馬具全体を指す)　⓬cinch: (鞍を止める)鞍帯　⓭plod: のろのろ進む　⓮nibble at . . .: 〜をかじる　⓯rein: 手綱　⓰jerk: 〜をぐいと引っぱる

間も馬具について学んだり、馬の世話のしかたを勉強したりしていた。

　1965年7月のある土曜の午後、父はモハーヴィ川まで出かけるべくヴァーティゴに鞍をつけた。私たちはみんな見物しに囲いまで出ていった。母までそばに来て、家の周りの日陰に生えているアイスプラントを鍬（くわ）で掘り起こしていた。父はまず、ヴァーティゴのたてがみと尻尾に櫛を入れた。するとヴァーティゴは、首をうしろに回して、囲いの柱に掛かっていたひづめ当てに何喰わぬ顔で唇を当てた。ひづめ当てが乾いた地面に落ちた。父はひるまず、ヴァーティゴのひづめの点検にかかった。馬はため息をつき、鼻をふふんと鳴らしてから、今度は柵から端綱（はづな）をはずしにかかった。そして何秒かすると、ぴょんぴょん跳んでその場を離れた。「ブルルルル」と父は、ぶらぶら揺れている端綱に手をのばしながらヴァーティゴに向かって小声でいなないた。ヴァーティゴを柱に縛り直してから、馬勒（ばろく）をつなぎ鞍を載せ留め具や鞍帯を留める作業に取りかかった。ヴァーティゴは鼻を鳴らし、体を揺すった。首をひょいと縦に振って、たてがみで父の顔をぴしゃりと叩いた。「ブルルルル」と父はくり返すばかりだった。やっとのことで準備が整った。暑く、乾いた日だった。午後3時くらいだったと思う。

　出発していく彼らの姿が目に浮かぶ——父はシャツも脱ぎジーンズにテニスシューズという格好、馬は顔を地面まで垂らしてのんびり進み、雑草をもぞもぞ嚙んだり、アリに向かって鼻を鳴らしたりしている。父は手綱（たづな）をしっかり引いて、ヴァーティゴは首をぐいと動かし白い

his head and swung his white mane in the air. I don't know what held all of us to the corral rails, or my mother to the ❶hoe and ice plant, but none of us moved. We watched them all the way down to the river, Vertigo's plodding and ❷stalling, my father's hitch of the reins, the ❸petulant sweep of the mane.

🎧032

Finally they were out of sight, over the edge of the desert and into a more forgiving place, the cool world of the Mojave River. We kids must have all wandered off then, to our cooler house, to our own concerns. I can't remember where I went then or what I did. I only remember that my mother called us back outside a couple of hours later. We stood in a line of six, our hands shading our eyes, searching the desert ❹terrain between our house and the river. I saw Vertigo prancing at an angle toward us, his head and tail held parade-proud, a breeze combing his mane. He seemed in no hurry to return; he just stopped and ❺grazed on weeds. He hadn't come far, and the river ❻glinted just on the other side of him. My stomach ached as I wondered if my father was hurt—❼bucked off and lying alone, full of pear cactus or, worse, red ants and scorpions. But then I saw him, running awkwardly in the soft sand toward Vertigo. The horse shook his head but continued to graze on the useless weeds. His saddle hung ❽precariously to the side.

---

❶hoe: 鍬　❷stall: ぐずぐずする　❸petulant: すねたような、不機嫌そうな　❹terrain: 地形、地勢　❺graze on . . .: (草)を食む　❻glint: きらっと光る　❼buck off . . .: (馬などが)(背に乗っているもの)を振り落とす　❽precariously: 不安定に、危なっかしく

たてがみを宙に振る。どうして私たちが誰も囲いの柵から離れなかったのか、どうして母が相変わらずアイスプラントを掘り起こしつづけたのかはよくわからない。でもとにかく誰一人動かなかった。父と馬がはるか向こうの川まで進んでいくのを私たちは見守った。ヴァーティゴはゆっくりと歩いてはぐずぐず止まり、父が手綱をぐいと引き、たてがみがうるさそうにさっと振られる。

　とうとうそんな姿も砂漠の彼方に消え、彼らはもっと穏やかな世界に、涼しいモハーヴィ川の世界に入っていく。私たち子供も、きっともうそのころには、涼しい家のなかに避難して、めいめいの用事にかまけていたにちがいない。そのとき自分がどこへ行ったのか、何をしたのか私には思い出せない。思い出せるのは、2時間ばかり経って、母がみんなを外に呼び戻したことだ。私たちは6人1列に並んで、手を額にかざし、家と川のあいだに広がる砂漠を見渡して父たちの姿を探した。と、ヴァーティゴが斜めの方角からこっちへ跳ねるように歩いてくるのを私は見つけた。頭も尻尾も、パレードに出ているみたいに誇らしげに掲げ、そよ風がたてがみに櫛を入れている。いっこうに急ぐ様子もなく、立ちどまってはまた雑草を食んでいる。まだそんなに近づいていなくて、川が馬のすぐ向こうでキラリと光った。父さんが怪我をしたんじゃないだろうか、そう思って私の腹が痛んだ。馬に振り落とされた父は、ナシサボテンで一杯の ── あるいはもっと悪いことに赤アリやサソリで一杯の ── 地面に一人横たわっている……。が、次の瞬間、父の姿が見えた。柔らかい砂地を、ヴァーティゴの方に向かってぎこちなく走っていた。馬は首を横に振ったが、依然無用の雑草を食みつづけている。鞍が脇腹に危なっかしくぶら下がっていた。

🎧 033

　My father approached, and I saw him ❶reach out for the reins. Vertigo swung his head away and pranced, not ❷in a beeline for home, but ❸angled, his head held erect, as if he knew we were watching. Just as suddenly, he again stopped and ❹yanked at weeds. My father, still standing where the horse had left him, dropped his arms and was frozen for a moment. Then, he strode again toward the animal. Again, Vertigo waited until my father was within arm's reach of the reins. This time, the horse jumped sideways, as if startled, and pranced off once again. We watched in silence. My mother leaned on her hoe and sighed.

🎧 034

　Vertigo ❺teased my father again and again, in a zigzag all the way up to the home stretch. By the fourth time he reached for and missed the swinging reins, I was sure he was frustrated and angry. He slapped at Vertigo's ❻rump as the horse ❼trotted off; I heard a thread of his weary voice ❽chastising the horse across the short distance between them, slowly coming closer to us.

🎧 035

　My mother must have slipped inside at that point; none of us noticed as we ❾worried my father up the slope of the desert. Finally, Vertigo pranced to the corral and stood waiting at the gate. He held his head high. His ❿nostrils were wide and his eyes were glinting. I felt my mother standing again beside me, along with my

---

❶ reach out for . . .: 〜をつかもうと手をのばす　❷ in a beeline: 一直線に　❸ angled: 角度をつけて、斜めに　❹ yank at . . .: 〜をぐいと引っ張る　❺ tease: 〜をからかう　❻ rump: (動物の) 尻　❼ trot: (馬などが) 早足で駆ける　❽ chastise: 〜をきつく叱る　❾ worry: 〜をたえず気にする　❿ nostril: 鼻孔

父が近づいていった。手綱に手をのばすのが見えた。ヴァーティゴはいきなりぐいっと首を振り、また跳ねるように歩き出した。まっすぐ棲みかに戻るのではなく、私たちに見られているのを意識しているみたいに頭をまっすぐ掲げ、斜めに歩いていた。そしてまたいきなり立ち止まって、雑草をくわえてぐいぐい引っぱった。父はといえば、馬に置き去りにされた場所に立ったまま、両腕を垂らし、しばし凍りついていた。やがて父は、どすどす大股で馬の方に歩き出した。ヴァーティゴは今度も手綱の届くところまで父が来るのを待った。そして今回は、ハッと驚いたように横っ飛びして、またしても跳ねるようにして立ち去った。私たちは無言で見守った。母は鍬に寄りかかってため息をついた。
　こうしてヴァーティゴは何度も父をからかってはジグザグに進み、とうとう囲いの近くまで戻ってきた。ぶらぶら揺れる手綱を取りそこなうのも4回目というあたりから、父は苛つき、怒っていたにちがいない。とっとっと走っていく馬の臀部を、父はピシャリと叩いた。少し距離を置いたまま、父と馬はのろのろこっちへ戻ってくる。その距離をはさんで、疲れたように馬を叱っている父の声が、風に乗って細々と聞こえてきた。
　母はこの時点で、もうこっそり家のなかに入っていたにちがいない。砂漠の斜面を歩く父のことが心配で、誰も気がつかなかったのだ。とうとうヴァーティゴが、囲いまで跳ねて戻ってきて、木戸のところに立って待った。頭は高く掲げていた。鼻の穴が広がり、目はギラギラ光っていた。いつの間にか母も、また私たち子供と並んで立っていた。みんな

brother and sisters, all of us silently watching my father walk the last stretch toward us.

🎧036

The closer he came, the worse I felt. He looked hot and sweaty. His shoulders stooped forward and his head was down. "What happened, Daddy?" my brother asked. Without answering, my father walked over and swung open the corral gate and stood back. Vertigo walked slowly inside and calmly ❶munched on hay. My father closed the gate and ❷latched it. He came and stood near us. There were beads of sweat caught in his eyebrows. "That's a pretty smart horse," he said, "You have to be one step ahead of old Vertigo."

🎧037

My mother held out a bottle of icy beer. No one spoke as he took a long sip. We all stood, looking down toward the river, the ❸Santa Ana wind whistling; no one looked over at Vertigo. But when we all turned to walk back toward the house, we heard his contented snort. Next Saturday, my father went back out in the corral, currying and saddling our new horse for another ride.

Janet Schmidt Zupan
Missoula, Montana

---

❶ munch on . . .: 〜をむしゃむしゃ食べる　❷ latch: 〜に掛け金をかける　❸ Santa Ana: サンタアナ（カリフォルニア州南部のサンタアナ山脈の斜面を吹き下ろす乾いた熱風）

何も言わずに、父がようやく私たちのもとに戻ってくるのを見守った。

　父が近づけば近づくほど、私の気まずい思いは募っていった。父は暑そうで、汗をかいていた。両肩が前に垂れ、首もうなだれている。「どうしたの、父さん？」と兄が訊いた。父は答えずに囲いまで歩いていき、木戸をぐいっと開(あ)けて、身をうしろに引いた。ヴァーティゴは悠々と中に入って、落ち着き払った顔で乾草をむしゃむしゃ噛んだ。父は木戸を閉じて、掛け金を掛けた。そしてこっちへやって来て、私たちのそばに立った。汗の玉が眉毛に引っかかっていた。「なかなか賢い馬だよ。ああいう奴は、一歩先を読まんといかんな」

　母が冷えたビールを差し出した。父がぐいぐい飲むあいだ、誰も何も言わなかった。サンタアナの熱風がひゅうひゅう鳴るなか、私たちはみな川の方を向いていた。誰もヴァーティゴの方を見ようとはしなかった。けれども、みんなで家のなかに戻っていくとき、ヴァーティゴが満足げに鼻を鳴らすのが聞こえた。次の土曜日、父はふたたび囲いに出て、もう一度乗馬に出かけようと、わが家の新しい馬に櫛を入れ、鞍をつけていた。

　　　　　　　　　　　　　　ジャネット・シュミット・ズーパン
　　　　　　　　　　　　　　モンタナ州ミズーラ

🎧038-053

OBJECTS

物

🎧039

A BICYCLE STORY

During the 1930s in Germany, every child's greatest hope was to own a bicycle. I saved up for years, putting aside the money I was given for birthdays and ❶Chanukah, along with the occasional reward for exceptionally good grades. I was still ❷shy of my goal by about twenty marks. On the morning I turned thirteen, I opened the door of the living room and was shocked to see the bicycle I had admired for so long in Mr. Schmitt's shop window. It had a wide black seat and a gleaming chrome frame. But best of all, it had wide red ❸balloon tires—the newest of inventions, which, contrary to the conventional narrow black tires, gave you more ❹traction and made the ride smoother. I could barely wait for the school day to end so I could ride it all over town, glorying in the admiration of passersby.

🎧040

The bicycle became my trusted companion. Then, one frosty January morning in 1939, I had to flee Germany and the Hitler regime. I was part of a hastily organized children's transport to England. We were only allowed one small suitcase, but my parents assured me they would somehow find a way to send my bike. Meanwhile, it would be stored safely in the cellar.

※トラック038をはじめ、オースターによる導入のナレーションのスクリプトは、232〜235ページにまとめて掲載されています。
❶Chanukah: ハヌカー（ユダヤ教の祭日期間。キリスト教のクリスマス同様に重要な祭り。Hanukkah ともつづる）　❷shy of . . .: 〜に足りない　❸balloon tire: バルーンタイヤ（幅広・低圧で凸凹道に強い）　❹traction: 牽引力

自転車物語

　1930年代のドイツでは、すべての子供たちの夢は自転車を持つことだった。私もやはり、何年もお金を貯めた。誕生日やハヌカーのお祝いも、特にいい成績を取ったときにもらったご褒美も、いっさい使わずに貯めたけれど、それでもまだ目標額に20マルクばかり足りなかった。13歳になった日の朝、居間のドアを開けると、驚いたことに、私がずっと前からシュミットさんの店のウィンドウでほれぼれと眺めてきた自転車がそこにあった。サドルは黒くて大きく、フレームはぴかぴかのクローム製。でも何よりいいのは、幅の広い赤いバルーンタイヤだった。当時の最先端を行く、いままでの細い黒のタイヤよりずっと牽引力が強く乗り心地も滑らかなタイヤだ。その日一日、学校が終わるのが待ち遠しくてならなかった。一刻も早く、通りがかる人たちの羨望のまなざしを浴びながら街じゅうを乗り回したかった。

　自転車は私の親友になってくれた。やがて、1939年1月のある凍てつく朝、私はヒトラーの支配するドイツから逃げ出す破目になった。あわただしく組織された〈子供たちを英国へ送る会〉に私も組み込まれたのだ。携帯を許されたのは小さなスーツケース一つだけだったが、何とかして自転車も送ると両親は約束してくれた。ひとまずは地下室にしまっておくからね、と両親は言った。

🎧 041

By ❶a stroke of luck, newfound friends were active in the Methodist Church of Ashford, Middlesex. They convinced their ❷congregation to raise funds to rent a flat for my parents, which, after official approval, would offer them a ❸haven in Great Britain. With these preliminary papers, the German government let my parents ship a large wooden crate to my friends. Each item had to be approved: no valuables were allowed, but they did not object to my bike. Meanwhile, my parents' papers were ready at the British ❹Home Office. Everything was ❺in order except for one last signature. Then war broke out, and my parents' fate was sealed. They both lost their lives in ❻camps in 1942.

🎧 042

In September 1939, all this was still in the future. One continued to hope for an early end to the war and to be reunited with one's family. A month later, I was accepted at a school where I would be trained as a children's nurse. St. Christopher's had moved from London—and the potential threat of bombs—to a small ❼hamlet in the south of England. After six months I received permission to take a week's holiday. I had to follow ❽protocol and label all the belongings I was not taking with me. I dutifully tagged my bike and left it in its ❾accustomed spot in the bike rack.

🎧 043

A few days later I received a letter from the ❿matron that a new

---

❶a stroke of luck: 思いがけない幸運　❷congregation: 信徒たち　❸haven: 避難所　❹Home Office: 内務省　❺in order: 整って、揃って　❻camp: 収容所　❼hamlet: 小さな村　❽protocol: (軍隊などでの)慣習、儀礼　❾accustomed: いつもの　❿matron: (学校などで)子供や生徒を管理する女性

幸いにも、私の世話をしてくれた人たちはミドルセックスのアシュフォード・メソジスト教会で活動していて、信徒たちに言って回って、私の両親のためのアパートを借りる金を集めてくれた。これで正式に認可さえ下りれば、両親もイギリスに避難できる。こうして送られてきた予備書類のおかげで、両親は私の世話をしてくれている人たちに宛てて、大きな木箱を送る許可をドイツ政府から取りつけた。送る品は一つひとつ認可を得ないといけない。貴重品は不可。でも自転車にはクレームはつかなかった。その間、英国内務省では両親の書類もほぼ出来上がった。あとはもう、サインひとつを残すのみ。が、まもなく戦争が勃発し、両親の運命はいっぺんに閉ざされた。二人とも1942年、強制収容所で死んだ。

　だが1939年9月には、両親の最期もまだ未来に属している。戦争が早く終わってまた家族が一緒になれるものと、みんなまだ期待していた。1カ月後、私は小児科の看護師の養成学校への入学を認められた。セント・クリストファー校と呼ばれるこの学校は、ロンドン空襲の危険を逃れて、イングランド南部の小さな村に移ってきていた。半年が過ぎて、私は1週間の休暇許可をもらった。ルールに従って、置いていく荷物にはすべてラベルを貼らないといけない。言われたとおり自転車にも札をつけ、バイクラックの定位置に置いていった。

　何日か経って、校長から手紙が来て、新しい法律が可決されたと知ら

law had been passed. I was now an "❶Enemy Alien." I could not be allowed within fifteen miles of the coast. Not only had my training come to a sudden ❷halt, but I was also told that I had not ❸complied with instructions and that none of my clothes could be found. As for my bicycle, they doubted that it even existed. I was furious, angry, and helpless ❹in the face of such outrageous lies, but most of all I missed my bike, which had been such a good friend.

🎧044

Over the next few years, I moved around a great deal, always complying with the law that required ❺refugees to register with the local police whenever they were gone from their residence for more than twenty-four hours. In late 1945, when I was living in London, I received a postcard with an official police seal on it. It threw me into a panic. The card instructed me to ❻report to the station as soon as possible. I trembled uncontrollably. What had I done wrong? Unable to cope with the fear and suspense, I immediately headed up the hill to the station and showed the card to the ❼sergeant on duty.

"Hey, Mac. Here's the girl you've been waiting for!"

Another officer appeared. "Did you ever own a bicycle?"

"Yes."

"What happened to it?"

🎧045

I told him the story. After a while, nearly everyone in the station

---

❶ enemy alien: 敵性外国人（戦時国に居住する敵国籍の外国人）　❷ halt:（行動・活動の）中止、停止　❸ comply with ...: 〜に従う　❹ in the face of ...: 〜に直面して、〜を突きつけられて　❺ refugee: 亡命者、難民　❻ report to ...: 〜に出頭する　❼ sergeant: 巡査部長（または広く警官一般を指す）

された。私はいまや「敵性外国人」であって、海岸から25キロ以内の場所に行ってはいけないという。看護師の勉強もあっけなく終わってしまった上、私が指示に従わなかったため衣類はいっさい見つからなかったと告げられた。自転車に関しては、そんなものが存在したことすら疑わしいと手紙には書いてあった。こんな法外な嘘をつきつけられて、私は憤り、怒り、絶望したが、何よりもまず、あんなにいい友だちだった自転車がなくなったことが悲しかった。

　その後何年かは、引越しの連続だった。そのあいだずっと、亡命者が住居を24時間以上離れる際は地元の警察に届けるべしという法律はちゃんと守っていた。1945年末、ロンドンに住んでいたときに、警察の正式印が押してある葉書が届いた。私はパニックに陥った。即刻警察署に出頭すべし、とそこにはあったのだ。体の震えが止まらなかった。私が何をしたというのだろう？　恐怖と不安に耐えきれず、私はすぐさま丘をのぼって警察署に駆けつけ、勤務中の巡査に葉書を見せた。

「おいマック、お待ちかねの娘さんが来たぞ！」

　もう一人の警官が現われた。「君、自転車を所有していたことがあるかね？」

「あります」

「どうなった、その自転車？」

　私は警官に一部始終を伝えた。話がはじまってしばらくすると、署内

was listening to me. I found that ❶puzzling.

"What did it look like?"

I described it. When I mentioned the unusual red balloon tires, they all laughed with relief. One of the officers ❷wheeled out a bike.

"Is this the one?"

It was ❸rusted, the tires were flat, and the seat had a ❹tear in it, but it was definitely my bicycle.

"Well, what are you waiting for? Take it home with you."

"Oh, thank you, thank you so much," I said. "But how did you ever find it?"

"It was abandoned, and someone found it. He ❺hauled it in because it still had a name tag on it."

🎧046

I wheeled it back to my apartment house full of happiness. When my landlady spotted me, however, she was horrified.

"You aren't going to ride that thing in London, are you?"

"Why not? It only needs a bit of repair and it'll be (as) good as new."

"It isn't that. Those wide tires are a ❻dead ❼giveaway that it's a German bike. The war is over, but we still hate those ❽bastards and everything that reminds us of them."

🎧047

I did have the frame painted, the seat and tires repaired, but a

---

❶puzzling: 不可解な　❷wheel: (車輪のついたもの) を押して動かす　❸rusted: さびついた　❹tear: 裂け目 ([tɛər]と読む)　❺haul: 〜を車で運ぶ　❻dead: 全くの、絶対の　❼giveaway: 素性を明かしてしまうもの　❽bastard: (悪い) やつ、野郎

のほぼ全員が私の話に耳を傾けていた。何だか妙だった。
「どういう見かけだったかね？」
　私はその外観を描写した。大きな特徴である、赤いバルーンタイヤのことを口にすると、みんなほっとしたように笑い声を上げた。そして、一人の警官が自転車を押してきた。
「これかね？」
　錆びついて、タイヤはパンクし、サドルには裂け目が入っていても、間違いなく私の自転車だった。
「さあ、何をぐずぐずしてる？　持って帰りなさい」
「ありがとうございます、本当にありがとうございます」と私は言った。「でもどうやって見つかったんですか？」
「捨ててあったのを誰かが見つけてくれたのさ。名札はとれていなかったから、届けてもらえたんだ」
　幸せ一杯の気持ちで、私はアパートまで自転車を押して帰った。ところが、大家さんの奥さんがそれに目をとめると、ぞっとしたような顔をした。
「あなたそれ、まさかこの街で乗るつもりじゃないでしょうね？」
「どうしていけないんです？　ちょっと修理すれば新品同様になりますよ」
「そういうことじゃないの。その幅広のタイヤで、一目でドイツ製だとわかってしまうのよ。戦争は終わったけど、みんなまだあの人非人たちを憎んでいて、あいつらを思い出させるものなんか見たくないのよ」
　フレームにペンキを塗ってもらい、サドルとタイヤも修理したけれ

single ride in my neighborhood was enough to convince me that my landlady was right. Instead of admiring stares, I got shouts and ❶jeers. Two years later, I sold it for a few ❷shillings to a collector of wartime ❸memorabilia.

Edith Riemer
Cherry Valley, New York

---

❶ jeer: あざけり　❷ shilling: シリング（英国の貨幣単位。1971年２月廃止。"a few shillings" は「はした金」という響き）　❸ memorabilia: 記念の品

ど、近所で一回乗っただけで、奥さんの言うとおりだとわかった。飛んできたのは、羨望のまなざしどころか、罵りの叫び、あざけりの声だったのだ。2年後、私は自転車を、戦時品のコレクターに二束三文で売った。

イーディス・ライマー

ニューヨーク州チェリーヴァレー

🎧049

THE STRIPED PEN

It was a year after World War II ended, and I was part of the Occupation Army in Okinawa. For the past few months, there had been several robberies in our base's yard area. Window screens had been cut, items in my ❶shack had disappeared—but strangely, the thief had taken nothing more than candy and little ❷doodads, nothing of real value. On one occasion, I had seen dried-mud prints of bare feet on the floor and wooden table. They were tiny and seemed to belong to a child. It was known that small bands of ❸orphaned kids ❹roamed the island ❺in packs, ❻living off whatever they could find, taking anything that was not ❼bolted down.

But then my prized ❽Waterman fountain pen disappeared. And that was ❾going too far.

🎧050

One morning, we picked up a man from the prisoner ❿compound. He was assigned to work duty. I had seen him several times before. He was quiet, he was handsome, he stood erect, he listened attentively. Looking at him, I imagined that whatever his rank in the Japanese army had been (possibly an officer), he had performed his duties well. And now, suddenly, there was my Waterman pen, clipped to the pocket of this dignified Japanese man.

---

❶shack: バラック　❷doodad: どうでもいいようなもの　❸orphaned: 孤児になった　❹roam: ～をうろつき回る　❺in packs: 群れをなして　❻live off...: ～を得てどうにか生きる　❼bolt down...: ～をボルトで締める　❽Waterman:（商標）ウォーターマン（米国製の万年筆）　❾go too far:（礼儀・常識などで）度を越す　❿compound: 囲い地

縞の万年筆

　第二次大戦が終わった翌年、私は占領軍の一員として沖縄にいた。それまでの何カ月か、基地構内で何度か盗難事件が起きていた。網戸がナイフで切られ、私のバラックに置いてあった物もいくつかなくなったが、妙なことに泥棒は、菓子だの何だのといったどうでもいい物しか盗んでいかなかった。あるとき、床や木のテーブルの上に裸足の足跡がついて、乾いた泥がこびりついていた。すごく小さな、子供の足とおぼしき跡だった。みなし児のグループが群れをなして島中をうろつき、しっかり固定されていない物は何であれ手当たり次第盗んで生き延びているという話はみんな聞いていた。

　ところがその後、私が愛用していたウォーターマンの万年筆がなくなった。こうなると放ってはおけない。

　ある朝、捕虜の居住区域から、作業任務に当たらせようと一人の男を徴用した。私もいままでに何度か見かけた男で、物静かな、顔立ちも端正で、背もしゃんとのびた、相手の話をきちんと集中して聞く男だった。この男を見ていると、日本軍でどんな階級だったにせよ（ひょっとすると士官だろうか）、軍人としてさぞ有能だっただろうと思った。と、突然、私のウォーターマンが目に飛び込んできた。この堂々とした日本人の、ポケットにささっていたのである。

🎧 051

I couldn't believe that he would steal. I was usually a good judge of character, and this man had impressed me as reliable. But I must have been wrong this time. After all, he had my pen, and he had been working in our area for several days. I decided to act on my suspicions and ignore the compassion I felt for him. I pointed to the pen and held out my hand.

He drew back, surprised.

🎧 052

I touched it, and again asked him, by gesture, to hand it over. He shook his head. He seemed slightly afraid—and totally sincere as well. But I wasn't going to let myself be ❶scammed. I put on an angry face and insisted.

Finally, he gave it to me, but with great sadness and disappointment. After all, what can a prisoner do if a ❷representative of the conquering army gives him an order? Punishments had been ❸meted out for refusing to obey, and he must have ❹had his fill of that kind of thing.

He didn't come back the next morning, and I never saw him again.

🎧 053

Three weeks later, I found my pen in my room. I was horrified by the ❺atrocity I had committed. I knew the hurt of being victimized—of being ❻unjustly outranked, of watching a trust killed in

---

❶scam: 〜をだます、ぺてんにかける　❷representative: 代表者、一員　❸mete out . . . :（賞罰など）を与える　❹have one's fill of . . . : 〜をさんざん味わう　❺atrocity: 極悪非道　❻unjustly outrank . . . : 階級をかさに〜を不当に扱う

この男が盗みを働くとは信じられなかった。私は概して、人間の見きわめは得意な方である。この男は私の目に、信頼すべき人物と映った。だが今回は読み違いなのだろう。何といっても、相手は私の万年筆を持っていて、何日か前から敷地内で仕事をしていたのだ。私は自分の疑念に従い、共感の方は無視することにした。私は万年筆を指さし、片手を差し出した。

　相手は驚いた顔を浮かべ、あとずさりした。

　私は万年筆を触って、もう一度身ぶりで、渡せと伝えた。男は首を振った。少し怯えているようで、そして心底誠実そうに見えた。だが私もだまされる気はない。怒りの表情を顔に浮かべ、強硬に迫った。

　やっとのことで男は万年筆を渡したが、その顔には深い悲しみと失望が浮かんでいた。しょせん彼は捕虜である。占領軍の上官に命令されたら何ができよう？　命令にそむけば罰則が待っている。彼もその手のことはさんざん経験していたにちがいない。

　翌朝、男は戻ってこなかった。私は二度と彼を見かけなかった。

　3週間後、私の部屋で万年筆が見つかった。私はぞっとした。何とひどいことをしてしまったのだろう。不当に差別されることの痛みは私も知っている —— 階級をかさに不正な扱いを受ける痛み、信頼の念が冷

cold blood. I wondered how I could have made such a mistake. Both pens were green, with gold stripes, but on one the stripes were ❶horizontal; on the other, they were ❷vertical. To make matters worse, I knew how much more difficult it must have been for this man to ❸come by one of those prized American ❹artifacts than it had been for me.

Now, fifty years later, I don't have either one of those pens. But I wish I could find the man, so that I could apologize to him.

Robert M. Rock
Santa Rosa, California

---

❶ horizontal: 水平の　❷ vertical: 垂直の　❸ come by ...: 〜を手に入れる　❹ artifact: (自然物に対して) 人工品、製品

酷に踏みにじられるのを目のあたりにするつらさ。どうしてあんなあやまちを犯してしまったのか。万年筆はどちらも緑色で、金の縞が入っていたが、一本の方は縞が横に入っていてもう一本では縦に入っていたのだ。それに、男がこの貴重なアメリカ製品を手に入れるのはどれだけ大変だったことか。私にとってより、ずっと大切な品だったにちがいない。

　あれから50年が過ぎたいま、どちらの万年筆も手元に残っていない。だが、あの男を見つけることができたらと私は思う。見つけて、謝ることができたら、と。

ロバート・M・ロック
カリフォルニア州サンタローザ

🎧 054-091

FAMILIES

家族

🎧055

RAINOUT

The last time I went to ❶Tiger Stadium (then known as Briggs Stadium) I was eight years old. My father came home from work and announced that he was taking me to the ball game. He was a fan, and we had gone to several day games before, but this would be my first night game.

🎧056

We got there early enough to park on Michigan Avenue for free. In the second inning, it started to rain, and then the rain turned into a ❷downpour. Within twenty minutes, they announced over the loudspeaker that the game had been canceled.

We walked under the stands for about an hour waiting for the rain to ❸let up. When they stopped selling beer, my father said that we should make a run for the car.

🎧057

We had a black 1948 sedan, and the door on the driver's side was broken and could only be opened from the inside. We got to the door on the passenger's side ❹panting and soaking wet. As my father ❺fumbled for the keys, they dropped out of his hand and fell into the ❻gutter. When he bent down to ❼retrieve them from the rushing water, the door handle knocked the brown ❽fedora off his head. I caught up with the hat about halfway down the block and

---

※トラック054をはじめ、オースターによる導入のナレーションのスクリプトは、232〜235ページにまとめて掲載されています。
❶Tiger Stadium: タイガー球場（ミシガン州デトロイトにあるスタジアム。1912年からアメリカン・リーグのデトロイト・タイガースの本拠地）　❷downpour: 土砂降り　❸let up:（雨・雪が）やむ　❹pant: 荒い息をする、息を切らす　❺fumble for . . . : 〜を探して手探りする　❻gutter: 道路の排水溝　❼retrieve: 〜を取り戻す　❽fedora: フェルト製の中折れ帽

雨天中止

　タイガー球場（当時はブリッグズ球場と呼ばれていた）に最後に行ったのは、8歳のときだ。仕事から帰ってきた父が、私を野球の試合に連れていってくれると宣言したのだ。父は野球ファンで、デーゲームには何度か連れていってもらっていたが、ナイトゲームはこれが初めてだった。

　早めに着いたので、ミシガン・アベニューに無料で駐車できた。2回から雨が降りだし、土砂降りになった。20分もしないうちに、拡声器を通して、試合中止が告げられた。

　雨が上がるのを待って、父と一緒にスタンドの下を1時間ばかり歩きまわった。ビールの販売が終わった時点で、車まで走っていこう、と父が言った。

　うちの車は黒い1948年型セダンで、運転席側のドアは壊れていて中からしか開かなかった。私たちははあはあ言いながら、ずぶぬれで助手席側のドアにたどり着いた。父がごそごそ鍵を探すうち、鍵が手から落ちて、道端の溝に落ちた。勢いよく流れる水から鍵を拾い上げようと父がかがむと、ドアの取っ手が茶色のフェルトの中折れ帽を父の頭から叩き落とした。半ブロックほど先まで行って私は帽子に追いつき、全速力

then raced back to the car.

🎧 058

My father was already sitting behind the ❶wheel. I jumped in, ❷collapsed onto the passenger's seat, and dutifully handed him the hat—which now looked like a wet rag. He studied it for a second and then put it on his head. Water poured out of the hat, splashing onto his shoulders and lap and then onto the steering wheel and dashboard. He ❸let out a loud ❹roar. I was frightened because I thought he was ❺howling with anger. When I realized he was laughing, I joined in, and for the next little while we just sat there in the car, laughing hysterically together. I had never heard him laugh like that before—and I never did again. It was a ❻raw explosion that came from somewhere deep within him, a force that he had always kept ❼dammed up.

Years later, when I spoke to him about that night and how I remembered his laughter, he insisted that it had never happened.

Stan Benkoski
Sunnyvale, California

---

❶ wheel:（車の）ハンドル（steering wheel）　❷ collapse:（人が）倒れる、へたり込む　❸ let out . . . :（声など）を出す　❹ roar: うなり声、叫び声　❺ howl: うなる、わめく　❻ raw: 生々しい　❼ dam up . . . :（感情など）を抑える、せき止める

で車に戻った。

　父はすでに運転席に座っていた。私は車に飛び込んで助手席に倒れ込み、父にうやうやしく帽子を渡した。帽子はいまやもう濡れ雑巾のようだった。父は一瞬帽子を見つめてから、頭に載せた。中から水が流れ出し、まず父の肩と膝にはねてから、ハンドルとダッシュボードにはねかかった。父は大声で吠えた。怒ってどなったのだと思ったので、私は縮み上がった。笑い声だとわかると、私も笑い出して、しばらくは二人ともそのまま狂ったように笑い転げた。父がそんなふうに笑うのを聞くのは初めてだった —— そして最後だった。それは父のどこか奥深くから出てきた、生々しい爆発だった。父がそれまでずっと抑えていた力だった。

　何年も経ってから、父にその晩のことを話して、父の笑い声をよく覚えていると私は言ったが、そんなことはなかったと父は言い張った。

スタン・ベンコスキー
カリフォルニア州サニーヴェイル

🎧060

TAKING LEAVE

For the last fifteen years I've been ❶confined to a nine-by-seven cage of solid steel bars, squeezed between walls I can touch with my fingertips if I stretch my arms. On my right is my bed. Its mattress is as flat as a pancake, and next to it is a ceramic toilet which is covered with a wooden board to keep the ❷stench out.

🎧061

I was in bed, ❸on the verge of falling asleep, when my ❹cell gate ❺cracked. Any time it opened was a welcome relief. I jumped up, stepped out on the ❻gallery, and called to the officer at the control booth a hundred feet away.

🎧062

"The ❼chaplain wants to see you. Get dressed," he said. I laced my boots, ❽snatched my jacket, and hurried outside. A call from the ❾cleric's office usually meant bad news. As I ❿whizzed past my neighbor's ⓫crib I heard him say, "Is everything all right, Joe?"

"I hope so," I said. "I think I'm going to make an emergency phone call."

🎧063

As I hurried across the snow-covered yard, groups of prisoners ⓬huddled together against the freezing wind. Blacks, whites, and ⓭Latinos ⓮bundled in multi-colored hoods, hats, gloves and mit-

---

❶confine: 〜を閉じ込める　❷stench: 悪臭　❸on the verge of . . .: 〜間際の、今にも〜しようとして　❹cell: (刑務所の)独房　❺crack: するどい音を立てる　❻gallery: 廊下　❼chaplain: (刑務所の)教戒師　❽snatch: 〜をひったくる、さっと取る　❾cleric: 聖職者、牧師　❿whiz: 素早く動く　⓫crib: (一般に)狭い場所、部屋　⓬huddle together: 群れ集まる、身を寄せあう　⓭Latino: ラテンアメリカ系住民　⓮bundled in . . .: 〜に包まれて

別れを告げる

　この15年間、頑丈な鉄棒でできた、縦2メートル70、横2メートル10の檻に閉じ込められてきた。腕を伸ばせば、指先が両側の壁に当たる。右手にはベッド。マットレスはパンケーキのように平たく、その隣に陶器のトイレがあり、悪臭が広がらないよう板がかぶせてある。

　ベッドで横になっていたら、寝入りばなに独房の入り口が開いた。戸が開くのは、いつでも大歓迎の息抜きだ。飛び起きて、廊下に出て、30メートル先の制御室にいる看守に声をかけた。

　「教戒師が会いたがっている。着替えるんだ」と看守は言った。俺はブーツのひもを結び、上着をつかんで大急ぎで外へ出た。聖職者からの電話は、たいてい悪い報せを意味する。隣人の住みかを足早に過ぎると、奴の声が聞こえた。「大丈夫か、ジョー？」

　「だといいんだが」と俺は言った。「緊急の電話をかけることになりそうだな」

　雪で覆われた庭を急ぎ足で横切ろうとすると、凍てつく風に身を寄せあっている囚人たちのグループが見えた。黒人、白人、ラテン系の連中が、いろんな色のフード、帽子、手袋、ミトンに身をくるんでいる。そ

tens. Some were familiar, but most were just faces in a vast sea of lonely insignificance. A few walked endless laps around the yard, others stared at one of the four TVs. Most were lost in self-imposed ❶distractions, doing the best they could to kill time the only way they knew how.

🎧064

At the wire gate leading to the guidance unit, I ❷shoved my pass into the tiny slot of the guard's wooden ❸shack. The officer ❹scrutinized it like a suspicious cashier looking at a ❺counterfeit fifty-dollar bill. Then, ❻dismissing me like a foreigner at a border crossing, he said, "Go ahead." Relieved, I sprinted toward the building. At last I was going to speak with my grandmother, a tough eighty-year-old lady who could ❼curse you out in a minute if you got her angry.

🎧065

We had not spoken in several weeks, because my father, who had just completed a ten-year federal sentence, had disconnected the three-way service at ❽Nan's house as a condition of his ❾parole. When I spoke to my father, he said, "Your grandmother's in the hospital, but she should be back in three days."

Although her health was ❿deteriorating, I never expected such a sudden decline. I remembered our last conversation, when she had cried and complained about her swollen legs.

"Nan, you got to try and walk around, stretch your legs and get

---

❶distraction: 気晴らし　❷shove: 〜を押し込む　❸shack: 小屋　❹scrutinize: 〜をじっくり調べる　❺counterfeit: 偽の　❻dismiss: 〜を行かせる　❼curse: 〜に悪態をつく、〜をののしる　❽Nan: おばあちゃん　❾parole: 仮釈放　❿deteriorate: 悪化する

のうち何人かは見覚えがあったが、ほとんどは、孤独な無意味さが作り出す大海に浮かぶ単なる顔に過ぎない。何人かは庭を果てしなく歩き回り、4台のテレビのどれかに見入ってる奴もいた。大半はみずからに課した気晴らしにのめり込んでいた。自分たちの知る唯一の方法で時間をつぶそうと、精一杯がんばっている。

案内所へつながる金網の入り口で、守衛がいる木造の小屋の細長い窓口に通行許可証を差し込んだ。偽50ドル札を目にして怪しいぞと思っているノジ係のように、守衛は許可証をじろじろ見た。それから、国境で外国人を通過させるように「行け」と言った。ほっとして、全力で建物めざして走っていった。ついに祖母と話せる。祖母はタフな80歳の、怒らせれば罵倒しまくって相手の息の根を止められる人物。

この何週間か、祖母と話していなかった。連邦裁判所の10年の刑期を終えたばかりの親父が、仮釈放の条件として、おばあちゃんの家の電話の三方向サービスを止めさせられたからだ。親父と話したときは、「おばあちゃんは入院しているが、3日で戻るはず」とのことだった。

祖母の健康状態はだんだん衰えてはいたが、これほど急激とは予想していなかった。最後に交わした会話を思い出す。祖母は泣きながら、腫れてしまった脚のことを愚痴っていた。

「おばあちゃん、歩こうとしなきゃだめだよ。脚を伸ばして、ちっと

some exercise," I ❶pleaded.

"I do. You don't understand. My legs are no good anymore. Last week I went to the bank and fell down on the sidewalk."

🎧066

I tried to ease her pain by talking about the good old days, when we lived on Ninety-eighth Street, and when Grandpa was alive. I pictured myself in the kitchen, watching her open the oven to ❷peek at the golden-brown loaves of Sicilian bread she baked for me and my grandfather. Back then one of my favorite treats was a hot round loaf of homemade bread stuffed with chicken roll and washed down with a tall glass of milk. Those were great times, and now, here I was, ❸clinging to them the same way my grandmother was.

🎧067

But even as we spoke about the happy times, she had still cried bitterly. Her greatest fear was that she'd be forced to live in an old-age home.

"I want to die in my own house. I don't want to live with strangers."

"Nan, I promise no one's going to ❹stick you in a home. Don't worry, when I get out I'll take care of you."

"Did you talk to the lawyer?"

"Yes, they're still working very hard."

"I hope to God you come home before I ❺go."

---

❶plead: 頼み込む　❷peek at . . . : 〜をそっとのぞく　❸cling to . . . : 〜にしがみつく　❹stick: 〜を押し込む　❺go: 死ぬ

は運動しなくちゃ」と俺は頼み込むように言った。

「してるよ。お前はわかってないんだよ。あたしの脚は、もう利かないの。先週、銀行に行って、舗道で転んじゃったよ」

俺は古き良き時代のことを話して、おばあちゃんの苦痛を和らげようとした。みんなで98丁目で暮らして、おじいちゃんもまだ生きていたころのこと。あの台所にいる自分の姿を俺は思い描いてみせた。おばあちゃんがオーブンを開けて、俺と祖父のために焼いてくれている、黄金色のシチリアのパンの焼け加減を見ている姿を俺は眺めている。あのころ俺が一番好きだったのは、チキン・ロールを詰めたほかほかの丸い自家製パンを、のっぽのグラスになみなみ注いだ牛乳で流し込むこと。最高の日々だった。そしていま、俺はここで祖母と同じようにあのころの思い出にしがみついている。

だが、幸せだったころを二人で語りあいながらも、祖母はひどく泣いた。祖母が何より恐れているのは、老人ホーム暮らしを強いられることだった。

「あたしゃ自分の家で死にたいよ。赤の他人とは暮らしたくない」

「おばあちゃん、俺が約束するよ、誰もどっかのホームに突っ込んだりしないよ。心配すんなよ。俺が出たら、面倒見るから」

「お前、弁護士さんと話したのかい」

「うん。みんな相変わらず一生懸命やってくれてるよ」

「あたしが逝く前にあんたが帰ってこれるといいねえ」

"I will, Nan, you just take care of yourself." Although I was able to reassure her, my feelings of guilt ❶lingered in my mind like the taste of spoiled milk.

🎧 068

Now, as I arrived at the chaplain's office, an officer said, "The ❷imam wants to see you." The imam? I said to myself. Randazzo, my counselor, must have made arrangements with him to call my grandmother. Inside the small room, four Muslims were busy filling tiny bottles with scented oils. The room smelled like jasmine, musk, and coconut ❸incense, ❹penetrating and ❺pungent, like the fragrance of ❻head shops in the '60s. Imam Khaliffa was talking on the telephone. He removed the receiver from his ear and cupped the mouthpiece. In a soft voice he told the men to leave the room.

🎧 069

As they ❼filed past me, he continued talking on the phone while I impatiently scanned the room. Although his desk was ❽cluttered with bottles and papers, my eyes were drawn to one particular document that seemed ❾out of place. On it I noticed my name written in bold letters above my grandmother's. It was a business letter from the Francisco Funeral Home.

🎧 070

The imam hung up the phone, and I asked, "What's going on?"
"Your brother Buddy called. He needs to speak with you."
Two days later, at 6:00 a.m., I was awakened by a young officer

---

❶linger: ぐずぐず残る　❷imam: イマーム（モスクで集団礼拝を先導する人）　❸incense: 香　❹penetrating: つんと鼻をつく　❺pungent:（鼻・舌を）刺すように刺激する　❻head shop: ドラッグ関連の品を売る店　❼file: 一列で進む　❽cluttered: 雑然とした　❾out of place: 場違いの

「帰るよ、おばあちゃん。体を大事にしろよ」。祖母を安心させることはできたが、饐えた牛乳の味みたいにやましい思いが心に残った。

　教戒師のオフィスに着くと、看守が言った。「イマームが会いたいそうだ」。なんでイマームが？　きっと俺のカウンセラーのランダーツォが、祖母に電話する件でイマームとも話をつけてくれたんだろう。小さな部屋のなかではイスラム教徒4人が、せっせと小瓶に香油を詰めていた。部屋はジャスミン、ムスク、ココナッツのお香の匂いがした。つんと鼻をつく匂いが充満している。60年代のドラッグショップみたいな香りだった。イマーム・カリファは電話中だった。俺を見ると、耳から受話器を外して、送話口を手でふさいだ。小声で男たちに、部屋から出るよう言った。

　男たちが一列になって俺の前を過ぎていくあいだ、イマームは電話で話しつづけ、俺はいらいらしながら部屋のなかを見渡した。イマームの机の上はビンと紙で散らかっていたが、場違いに見える書類に目が吸い寄せられた。太字で俺の名前が書いてあって、その下に祖母の名前があった。フランシスコ葬儀会館からのビジネスレターだった。

　イマームが電話を切ると、俺は訊ねた。「何事なんです？」

「弟さんのバディから電話があった。話があるそうだ」

　2日後の午前6時、俺はリゾという若い看守に起こされた。痩せてい

named Rizzo. He was thin, had ❶short-cropped black hair, and a voice that spoke with the soothing calm of a priest in a ❷confessional booth. Perhaps he also knew what it felt like to experience the loss of a loved one. I was grateful.

🎧071

When we crossed the yard, it was windy, dark, and pouring with rain. Inside the administration building, a ❸burly Irishman with blond hair and rosy cheeks approached me and said, "I'm sorry to hear about your grandmother." I put on the ❹garments given to me by the prison for the trip: blue jeans, a white shirt, and a tan jacket. I wore my own sneakers. I glanced at myself in the mirror and was disgusted by my reflection.

🎧072

At last we climbed into a specially equipped van with a thick ❺Plexiglas partition separating me from the officers, who carried .38-❻caliber pistols strapped to their hips in black leather holsters. My legs were ❼shackled by a twelve-inch dog chain, secured tightly at each ankle. I was also handcuffed with a belly chain. This was fastened to my cuffs with a master lock. To eat I had to bend forward and strain my neck to ❽peck at a sandwich ❾clasped in my fingers.

🎧073

I had not been outside the stone walls of the prison for fifteen years. We drove past mountains, trees, and farms with black-and-

---

❶short-cropped:（髪など）短く切り詰めた　❷confessional booth: 懺悔室　❸burly: がっしりした　❹garment:（複数形で）衣類　❺Plexiglas:（商標）プレキシガラス（きわめて頑丈で飛行機の窓などに使われる）　❻caliber:（銃身の）口径　❼shackle: 〜にかせを掛ける　❽peck at . . . : 〜をちびちび食べる　❾clasp: 〜を握り締める

て、刈り込んだ黒い髪、懺悔室の司祭のような、人をなだめる冷静さを
もった声の男だ。愛する者を失うという体験がどんなものか、リゾも
知っていたのかもしれない。ありがたかった。

　二人で庭を突っ切ると、風は強く、空は暗くて、土砂降りだった。管
理棟に入ると、金髪で赤々とした頰のがっしりしたアイルランド人が
やって来て、「ご愁傷さまです」と言った。この外出のために監獄から
与えられた衣類を俺は着た。ブルージーンズ、白いシャツ、褐色の上
着。スニーカーは自分のを履いた。鏡をちらっと見て、映っている自分
にうんざりした。

　やっとのことで、特別装備のバンに乗り込んだ。俺を看守たちと隔て
る、分厚いプレキシガラスの仕切がある。奴らは腰につけた黒革のホル
スターに38口径をさしている。俺の両脚には30センチのドッグチェー
ンがつながれ、両足首でしっかり固定されている。ベリーチェーンもか
けられて、腹のあたりに手首が固定されている。このチェーンが、マス
ターロックで手錠につながれている。食べるときは前にかがみ、首を伸
ばし、指につかんだサンドイッチをつつくのだ。

　監獄の石壁の外に出るのは15年ぶりだった。山々、木々、黒と白の牛
が草をのんびり食む農場を過ぎた。シュールな立体写真のなかにいる気

white cows ❶grazing leisurely on the grass. I felt like I was part of a ❷surreal three-dimensional photograph. Soon we entered a valley that was covered in thick fog. It ❸consumed us like the smoke in woods after a ❹smoldering forest fire. Suddenly a deer darted from the mist. It leapt onto the highway and into the front end of the pickup truck that was ahead of us. The driver didn't have a chance to ❺swerve. I ❻whipped my neck around and slid to the edge of my seat.

🎧074

"Did you see that?" Officer Warren asked.

I ❼peered out the side window, through beads of raindrops ❽scurrying across the glass, and saw the deer ❾sprawled on the ❿perimeter of the roadway. As I strained forward in my seat, my ⓫shackles and ⓬restraints dug deep into my flesh. The deer's tongue ⓭dangled from her soft furry jaw, and her mouth was slightly open as she ⓮exhaled nervous panting puffs of steam.

🎧075

"*It's still alive!*" I exclaimed.

"Yeah, but she don't look good," Officer Warren said. I wanted to see her sprint back into the woods. Instead she lay motionless, as still as the fog hanging over the valley, as stiff as the trees.

🎧076

By midafternoon trees were replaced by apartment houses and commercial brick buildings with an assortment of bubble-shaped,

---

❶graze:(牛などが)草を食む　❷surreal: シュールな　❸consume: 〜を消滅させる　❹smolder: くすぶる　❺swerve: 急にそれる、急に向きを変える　❻whip: 〜を急に動かす　❼peer: じっと見る、凝視する　❽scurry: 素早く動く　❾sprawled:(四肢をのばして)力なく倒れて　❿perimeter: 周囲、末端　⓫shackle: 手錠、手かせ　⓬restraint: 拘束道具　⓭dangle : ぶら下がる　⓮exhale:(息など)を吐く

分だった。まもなく、濃い霧に覆われた谷に入った。くすぶった山火事のあとで煙が森を包み込むみたいに、霧が俺たちを取り込んだ。と、霧のなかから鹿が一頭飛び出してきた。鹿は高速道路に飛び上がって、俺たちの前方を行く小型トラックに突っ込んだ。運転手はよける間がなかった。俺はさっと横を向いて、座席の端までずっていった。

「見たか？」とウォーレン看守が言った。

横の窓から外を見ると、ガラスを走る雨の滴ごしに、鹿が車道の端に力なく倒れていた。座席から身を乗り出すと、手かせ、足かせが体にぎゅっと食い込んだ。雌鹿の柔らかい、ふさふさ毛の生えたあごから舌がだらりと垂れて、口はわずかに開き、あえぐような息を不規則に吐いていた。

「まだ生きてる！」と俺は叫んだ。

「ああ、でも、だめだろうな」とウォーレン看守が言った。俺は鹿が森へ駆け戻るのを見たかった。だが鹿は横たわったままだった。谷にかかる霧のようにじっと動かず、木々のようにこわばって。

午後のなかごろには、木々に代わって、アパートや、丸みを帯びたさまざまな色の派手な太字が踊るレンガ造りの商業用ビルが見えてきた。

multicolored, bright bold letters. Some of the structures were ❶boarded up. Finally we exited Lexington Avenue, passed the piers of Manhattan, crossed the Brooklyn Bridge, and emerged on Atlantic Avenue. The city was vaguely familiar, dreamlike.

🎧077

I imagined myself in the old days, leaning on the armrest of my black 1983 Ninety-Eight ❷Oldsmobile. I'd be listening to music with a thick ❸joint burning in the ashtray. Inhaling the smoke of the sweet sticky ❹weed, its pungent aroma drifting through a crack in the ❺moonroof in swirling ❻plumes. Once I had had it all.

🎧078

On Atlantic Avenue there were rows of stores and ❼bodegas and people ❽buzzing everywhere. Beautiful women wearing tight pants, ❾platform shoes, and leather jackets strolled by, swinging shopping bags. They ❿swayed their hips ⓫in sync with the ⓬seductive rhythm and style that ⓭spelled ⓮attitude with a capital A in the ⓯barrio. There were furniture shops with sofas outside, a black homeless man begging, and an ⓰amputee in a wheelchair hurrying across the street.

🎧079

When we ⓱pulled up in front of the funeral home, Officer Warren said, "Hold on. I have to check it out."

Two minutes later he appeared and nodded to his partner. Then, with Rizzo's assistance, I carefully climbed out of the van. "Wait,"

---

❶board up ...: (空家など) に板を打ちつける　❷Oldsmobile: (商標) オールズモービル (米国 General Motors 社 Oldsmobile 事業所の製造する乗用車の総称)　❸joint: マリファナタバコ　❹weed: マリファナ　❺moonroof: ムーンルーフ (自動車の屋根につけた透明部分)　❻plume: もくもく立ち上る煙　❼bodega: 酒場　❽buzz: がやがや話す　❾platform shoe: プラットフォーム・シューズ (底が厚い靴)　❿sway: ～を (左右に) 揺する　⓫in sync with ...: ～と同調して、かみ合って　⓬seductive: 魅惑的な、セクシーな　⓭spell: ～を意味する、いかにも～を表している

建物のいくつかは板を打ちつけて閉め切ってあった。ついにレキシントン・アベニューを出て、マンハッタンの埠頭を過ぎ、ブルックリン橋を渡って、アトランティック・アベニューに出た。街はなんとなく知っているような、夢のなかの情景みたいだった。

　昔の自分を想像した。黒い、1983年型オールズモービル98の肘掛けに寄りかかっている。音楽を聴いていて、灰皿には火を点けた太いマリファナ。甘い、べたつくマリファナの煙を吸い込むと、鼻をつく香りが、うずを巻いて、ムーンルーフの隙間から漂い出る。かつて俺には何もかもあったのだ。

　アトランティック・アベニューには店とバーが建ち並び、どこも人が騒いでいた。美しい女たちが、ぴっちりしたパンツ、プラットホーム・シューズを履き、革ジャンを着て、買い物袋を揺らしながら、ぶらぶら歩く。魅惑的なリズムとスタイルで腰を振るその姿は、スペイン語街ではお洒落の代名詞だ。表にソファを出している家具屋があり、黒人のホームレスの男が物乞いをし、脚を切断した人が車椅子でそそくさと道を渡っていた。

　葬儀会館の前に車が停まると、ウォーレン看守が言った。「ちょっと待ってろ。確認してくる」

　2分後、彼が戻ってきて、相棒にうなずいてみせた。リゾに手伝ってもらって、俺はバンからそろそろと降りた。歩いていると、リゾが「待

---

❹ attitude with a capital A: とびきりお洒落なポーズ　❺ barrio: メキシコ人街、ヒスパニック居住地　❻ amputee: 手足を失った人　❼ pull up: 車を止める

Rizzo said, stopping me in midstride. "Let's take the belly chain and cuffs off first."

🎧 080

He inserted a key into the master lock and with a quick, practiced twist snapped it open. He reached around my back, unwrapped the chain, and then removed the handcuffs. I stretched and rubbed my wrists. They were swollen and red and had deep ❶creases in them. Followed by Rizzo, I ❷limped inside the lobby, taking slow, ❸even steps to avoid ❹tripping on the ❺tether still attached to my ankles.

🎧 081

My brother Buddy appeared. He was tall and broad and ❻impeccably dressed in a fine black suit. I could tell he was shocked and glad to see me. We shook hands and kissed. Then my uncle, whom I hadn't seen in fifteen years, ❼sauntered in. He looked much older, seemed shorter, and was as round as a wine barrel. He paused for a second, studying me the same way I ❽pondered him. Fifteen years was a long time.

🎧 082

"Joey," he said in his distinctive Sicilian ❾brogue.

I wrapped my arms around him. "It's great to see you, Uncle Charlie."

"I'm a grandfather now," he said, proudly slipping a photo from his wallet. "Your cousin Joey and his wife had a boy. His name is

---

❶crease: しわ ❷limp: 足をひきずる（ように歩く） ❸even: 一定の、規則正しい ❹trip on . . . : 〜につまずく ❺tether: つなぎ綱［鎖］ ❻impeccably: 申し分なく ❼saunter: ぶらぶら歩く ❽ponder: 〜をじっくり眺める ❾brogue: 地方なまり

て」と呼び止めた。「まずベリーチェーンと手錠を外そう」

　リゾはマスターロックに鍵を差し込むと、素早い、慣れたひねりでかちりと開けた。俺の背中に手を伸ばして巻かれていたチェーンを外し、手錠も外してくれた。俺は伸びをして、手首をさすった。両手首が腫れて赤くなり、深い溝が刻まれていた。リゾが後ろからついてきて、俺は足をひきずりながらロビーに入った。まだ両足首についている鎖を踏んで転ばないよう、ゆっくり、一定の歩幅で進んだ。

　弟のバディが現われた。背が高く、恰幅のいいバディは立派な黒のスーツを着て、非の打ちどころのない身なりだった。俺を見るのがショックでもあり、嬉しくもあることがわかった。俺たちは握手をして、キスをした。すると、15年会っていなかったおじが入ってきた。前よりずっと年を取って、背が低くなったように見えて、ワイン樽みたいに丸かった。おじは一瞬立ち止まり、俺がおじのことをあれこれ考えているのと同じように、俺のことをじっくり見た。15年は長い。

　「ジョーイ」とおじははっきりとわかるシチリアなまりで言った。

　俺はおじの体に両腕を回した。「チャーリーおじさん、会えて嬉しいよ」

　「もうじいちゃんなんだよ」とおじは誇らしげに財布から写真を取りだした。「お前のいとこのジョーイのとこに男の子がうまれたんだ。コ

Cologero."

🎧 083

I took the picture and glanced at it and wondered where all the years had gone. I remembered my cousin Joey when he was a teenager wearing a football jersey rushing out of his house in College Point to play ❶two-hand touch. Now he was a father. I handed the photo back to my uncle and said, "Congratulations."

🎧 084

I stepped into the viewing room and encountered my sisters, Gracie and Maria. Both were drowned in black clothes. We hugged and kissed and each cried on my shoulder. I was quickly surrounded by other family members, including my father, whom I had not seen in ten years. His hair was pure white and as fine as rabbit's fur.

🎧 085

"You made it," he said.

We embraced. "Yeah, Dad, security cleared me."

Because of restrictions, I had not spoken to my father while he was away. I stood there and scrutinized him, searching for the man I had last seen on a visit ten years ago. I knew I'd never find him again.

🎧 086

The room was still and quiet. Chairs lined one wall and a sofa the other. There were tables with lamps on them, and others that held crystal bowls filled with mints. At the rear of the room my grand-

---

❶ two-hand touch: ツーハンド・タッチ（タッチフットボールのこと。相手側のボール保持者に両手で触れるとダウンとなる）

ロジェーロっていうんだ」

　俺は写真を受け取って眺めた。あれだけの年月はどこへ行ったんだろう。いとこのジョーイがティーンエージャーだったころを覚えている。フットボールのジャージを着て、ツーハンド・タッチをして遊ぼうとカレッジポイントの家から飛び出していく姿。その彼もいまや人の親だ。俺は写真をおじに返して、「おめでとうございます」と言った。

　対面室に入って、姉と妹に会った。グレイシーもマリアも、喪服を着ていた。俺たちは抱きあい、キスをして、二人とも俺の肩で泣いた。俺はたちまち家族に取り囲まれた。10年ぶりに会う親父もいた。すっかり白髪になって、ウサギの毛みたいに細い髪だった。

　「来れたな」と親父が言った。

　親父と抱きあった。「うん。セキュリティが認めてくれたんだ」

　規制上、親父が刑務所に入っているあいだは、話すことができなかった。俺は立ちつくし、親父をつくづくと眺めた。そして10年前訪ねてくれたときに会った男の面影を探した。二度と見つからないことは充分承知しながら。

　部屋は静まり返っていた。一方の壁に沿って椅子が並び、もう一方の壁際にはソファがあった。ランプの載っているテーブルと、ミントを入れたクリスタルの器を置いたテーブルが何卓かずつあった。部屋の奥に

mother lay lifeless, surrounded by an assortment of colorful floral arrangements. As I approached I could smell the familiar fragrance of freshly picked roses. I placed my hand on the edge of her bronze ❶casket and gazed at her face. She was thinner than the last time I had seen her, five years ago. Her skin was pale and colored with a thick coat of makeup that made her look unnatural. She wore a smile that seemed more like a ❷contrived grin. On her wrist was the same gold bracelet that she always wore on special occasions. It was heavy and ❸adorned with several medals that jingled like bells when she walked. Now the charms—large solid-gold hearts and ❹diamond-studded medallions inscribed with dates and ❺heartfelt expressions—hung stiffly from her frozen wrist. She was dressed in a beautiful silk and lace pink gown that stretched to her ankles. On her feet she wore tiny pink shoes the color of seashells.

🎧087

All these years I had expected this day. I just never thought it would happen so ❻damn suddenly. Now all I had left were memories. Fragmented ❼remnants of our lives scattered on the lid of her coffin. One was a picture of my grandmother taken in 1984, the year I went away, standing by the dock of our home in Howard Beach. Boats adorned with flags, some with ❽fly bridges as tall as our house, floated on the surface of calm waters, waiting to cast off. She's wearing a pair of shorts and sneakers and has a huge grin on her face. And there beside her are the rosebushes she raised, explod-

---

❶casket:（通例装飾を施した）棺　❷contrived grin: わざとらしく作った笑み　❸adorned with ...: 〜で飾った　❹diamond-studded: ダイヤモンドをちりばめた　❺heartfelt expressions: 心のこもった言葉　❻damn: とても、ひどく　❼remnant: 断片　❽fly bridge: フライブリッジ（キャビンの上にあるスペース）

は、もう生きてはいない祖母が、色とりどりの花のアレンジメントに囲まれて横たわっていた。近づいていくと、摘みたてのバラの嗅ぎなれた香りが薫った。銅の棺のふちに手を載せて、祖母の顔を眺めた。5年前に会ったときより痩せていた。肌は青白く、分厚い化粧で覆われているせいで、不自然に見えた。浮かべている笑みは、わざとらしいにたにた笑いに見えた。手首につけた金のブレスレットは、特別な日にはいつも着けていた品だ。重たいブレスレットで、飾りにメダルがいくつもついていて、祖母が歩くと鈴のように鳴った。それがいま、大きな純金のハートの飾りや、日付や心尽しの言葉を刻んだ、ダイヤモンドをちりばめられたメダルは、冷たく硬直した手首から堅くぶら下がっている。祖母はきれいな絹とレースの、足首まであるピンクのガウンをまとっていた。足には小さなピンクの、貝殻色の靴を履いていた。

　この日が来るのは何年も前から覚悟していた。こんなに突然とは思いも寄らなかっただけだ。いまや残るのは思い出だけ。祖母の棺のふたに、俺たちの人生の断片が散らしてあった。そのひとつは、1984年に撮った祖母の写真。俺が刑務所に入った年だ。祖母はハワード・ビーチの家の船着き場の横に立っている。旗で飾りつけられたボートが穏やかな水面に浮かんで索が解き放たれるのを待っている。何隻かは、ブリッジが我が家くらい高い。祖母は短パンとスニーカーを履いて、満面の笑みを浮かべている。かたわらでは、祖母が手塩にかけたバラの茂みが、

ing in brilliant full bloom.

🎧088

　At our house my grandmother usually kept large bowls of warm food in the oven. Pans of chicken cutlets and pasta, or meat and white potatoes, were always available for visitors who wanted to sit down and eat. On Sundays Nan always cooked a huge meal, large pastel-colored bowls filled with pasta, ❶marinara sauce, garlic, and freshly picked basil. Then we passed around trays of meatballs, sausages, and meats stacked a foot high. I would wipe the sauce from my lips between mouthfuls of food and ❷gulps of red wine mixed with 7Up. My grandfather wore a napkin tucked into his shirt and a pen in his pocket; he would busily ❸grate a chunk of fresh ❹ricotta cheese onto his macaroni. His arm moved in round, sweeping, circular motions. When he was finished, I took the cheese from him and did the same.

🎧089

　When I used to come home after junior high school to a house filled with the aroma of sauce ❺simmering on the stove, I'd snatch a loaf of ❻semolina bread, tear off a ❼hunk, and soak it in the sweet red gravy. Before long, I'd hear my grandmother say, "Get outa here, will you?" She didn't say it in a ❽mean way, she said it proudly, delighted by the thought of how much I loved her cooking.

🎧090

　The time to leave arrived with a nod from Officer Warren. Every-

---

❶marinara sauce: マリナーラ・ソース（トマト、タマネギ、ニンニク、香辛料で作る）　❷gulp: ゴクゴク飲み込むこと　❸grate:（チーズや大根）を下ろす　❹ricotta: リコッタ（イタリアチーズの一種）　❺simmer: ぐつぐつ煮える　❻semolina: セモリナ（パスタ用の上質の小麦粉）　❼hunk:（パン・肉の）大きな塊　❽mean: 意地悪な

はじけたように見事に咲き誇っている。

　家では祖母はたいてい、温かい料理の深皿をオーブンに入れていた。チキンカツやパスタの平皿、じゃがいもを添えた肉などが、誰がいつ来ても腰をすえて食べられるよう常備してあった。日曜日にはおばあちゃんはいつも大量の食事を作っていた。パスタ、マリナーラ・ソース、ニンニク、摘みたてのバジルが山と盛られた、大きなパステルカラーのボウル。ミートボール、ソーセージ、肉が30センチも積まれた、何枚ものトレーを俺たちはまわす。食べ物を頬張っては、口からソースを拭って、セブンナップを混ぜた赤ワインを流し込む。ナプキンをシャツにたくし入れ、ポケットにペンを差している祖父は、新鮮なリコッタチーズをせっせと挽いて自分のマカロニにかける。祖父の腕はぐるぐると、大きな円を描いた。祖父が挽き終わると、俺がチーズをもらって、同じことをした。

　中学のころ、学校から帰ると、コンロの上でソースがことこと煮える匂いが家じゅうに満ちていて、俺はセモリナブレッドを一斤つかんで、大きな塊をちぎりとると、甘くて赤いソースに浸したものだ。ほどなく祖母の声がする。「出てお行き」。きつい言い方ではなかった。むしろ誇らしげな口ぶりだった。自分の手料理を俺がどんなに気に入っているかわかっていて、喜んでいたのだ。

　ウォーレン看守がうなずいて、帰る時間になった。別れのキスをしよ

one ❶surged forward to kiss me good-bye. My uncle and I grasped each other one last time, and he said, "You were your grandmother's world, she loved you more than anything." Then my father held me and exploded into a violent, ❷shuddering ❸convulsion of sobs. We stood there clinging to each other like passengers on a plane about to crash, ❹hurtling toward the ground. At that moment, with my dad's tears falling on my shoulder, I felt like I was his father and he was my son, and in the ❺solace of my arms he discovered the safety I had once sought in his.

🎧091

I walked to the van and extended my hands to Officer Rizzo to have the cuffs ❻clamped on my wrists again. Instead, he said, "We'll put them on later, after we eat." This surprised me. I hopped into the van, slid close to the window, and peered out one last time hoping to freeze this moment that would have to last as a picture in my mind forever. I watched my uncle reach into his jacket pocket, pull out a cigar, and light it up, taking short, quick puffs. As we rolled away, I waved to him and wondered if my expression ❼betrayed my sadness.

Joe Miceli
Auburn, New York

---

❶surge: 殺到する　❷shudder: 震える　❸convulsion: (怒り・笑いなどの) 激しい発作　❹hurtle: 突進する　❺solace: 安堵、慰め　❻clamp: 〜を固定する　❼betray: 〜をさらけ出す

うとみんなが押し寄せてきた。おじともう一度抱きあい、おじは言った。「お前はばあちゃんのすべてだった。お前を何より愛してたんだよ」。次いで俺を抱きしめた親父は、激しく身を震わせてしくしく泣き出した。いまにも墜落して、地面に叩きつけられようとしている飛行機の乗客のように、俺たちはたがいにしがみついた。親父の涙を肩に受けていると、まるで俺が父親で、親父が息子のように思えた。かつて俺が父の腕に求めた安らぎを、俺の腕のうちに親父が見つけたような気がした。

　バンまで歩いていって、ふたたび手錠がはめられるようリゾ看守に両手を差し出した。ところが、「あとでつけよう。食べてから」と彼が言った。驚いた。俺はバンに飛び乗り、窓際まで体を滑らせて、最後にもう一度、外を見た。記憶の映像に永遠に残さなくてはいけないこの一瞬を、何とかして焼きつけようと。おじが上着のポケットに手を入れ、葉巻をとり出して火を点け、みじかくプカプカと吹かすのを見ていた。車が走りだすなか、おじに手を振りながら、俺の顔は悲しみをさらしているだろうかと考えた。

ジョー・ミセリ

ニューヨーク州オーバーン

🎧 092-108

SLAPSTICK

スラップスティック

🎧 093

A FELT FEDORA

A felt ❶fedora always covered my father's short brown curls. He wore a gray one for work—sometimes small ❷kernels of wheat mingled with drops of tractor oil ❸nestled in the ❹brim. He had a brown one for dress and a beige one for leisurely Sunday drives or taking in a ❺Roy Rogers movie on a warm summer evening. We never went to the movies except in the summer, maybe because the days were long and hot or because the nights took too long to come or because the cool darkness of the Star Theatre ❻beckoned to my father after he had been ❼working the dusty, dry land.

🎧 094

My father never went anywhere without one of his hats. They hung outside the back kitchen door on pegs, lined up in a row. Same size, same shape, same smell—a mixture of ❽Old Spice, ❾Lifebuoy soap, and a touch of the ❿Brylcreem he used to ⓫tame his unruly hair.

🎧 095

He never wore one inside, but when he was outside it was on his head or in his hand. He'd ⓬tip it when greeting a lady and take it off when entering a building, even the post office. His manners were ⓭impeccable, but he wasn't comfortable without his hat. My

---

※トラック092をはじめ、オースターによる導入のナレーションのスクリプトは、232〜235ページにまとめて掲載されています。
❶ fedora: フェルト製の中折れ帽　❷ kernel:（小麦などの）穀粒　❸ nestled in . . .: 〜に収まっている　❹ brim:（帽子などの）つば　❺ Roy Rogers: ロイ・ロジャーズ（オハイオ州出身の俳優。歌うカウボーイ・スターとして多くの映画に出演）　❻ beckon to . . .: 〜を手招きする　❼ work: 〜を耕す
❽ Old Spice:（商標）オールドスパイス（米国 Shulton 社の男性用化粧品）　❾ Lifebuoy:（商標）ライ

フェルトの中折れ帽

　父の短くて茶色い巻き毛には、いつもフェルトの中折れ帽がのっていた。仕事に出かけるときはグレーのやつ———時おり、小さな小麦の粒がいくつか、トラクターオイルが落ちたしみと混ざって帽子のつばについていたものだ。よそゆきのときは茶色の帽子を、のんびりと日曜日のドライブに行くときや、暖かい夏の夕方にロイ・ロジャーズの西部劇を観に行くときは、ベージュのをかぶった。私たちが映画に行くのは夏だけだった。日が長くて暑かったからかもしれないし、夜が来るのが遅すぎたからかもしれないし、それともスター・シアターの涼しい暗闇が、埃っぽい乾いた土地で一日働いた父を手招きしていたからかもしれない。

　父が帽子なしで出かけることは絶対になかった。帽子は台所の戸の外に、一列に並べて掛けてあった。全部が同じサイズ、同じ形で、同じ匂いがした。オールドスパイスのオーデコロン、ライフブイ石鹸、それから、あのくせっ毛を押さえるのに使うブリルクリームの匂い。

　家にいるときは一度も帽子をかぶらなかった父だが、外にいるときはかならず頭の上か手のなかに帽子があった。女性に挨拶するときはひょいと持ち上げ、建物に入るときには、そこが郵便局であってもかならず脱いだ。父のマナーは申し分なかったが、帽子なしでは居心地が悪そう

フブイ（英国・米国製の石けん）　❿Brylcreem:（商標）ブリルクリーム（英国製のヘアクリーム）　⓫tame: 〜を制御する、慣らす　⓬tip:（帽子）を挨拶のために軽く持ち上げる　⓭impeccable: 申し分のない

mother made him leave it in the car when we went to the movies; he would have preferred holding it in his lap.

🎧 096

Many years later, my brother and I and our families were with my mother and father in a department store in Portland, Oregon. We were trying to help my father find a new hat. He tried them all on: wrong size, wrong color, brim too narrow, band didn't match. This went on and on, and the salesman was beginning to lose patience. My father finally found the perfect one and with a huge grin showed it to my mother. We all breathed a sigh of relief, until she looked at it and said, "Ted, you old fool, that's your own hat!"

Joan Wilkins Stone
Goldendale, Washington

だった。映画を観るときは、母に言われて車のなかに帽子を置いていった。父としては膝の上に載せておきたかったと思うが。

　何年もあとになって、弟と私はそれぞれの家族を引き連れ、母と父を誘って、オレゴン州ポートランドのデパートに出かけた。父の新しい帽子を探そうというのだ。父はそこにあった帽子を全部試したが、どれも気に入らなかった。サイズが合わない、色がよくない、つばが狭すぎる、ハットバンドの色がほかと合わない。これが延々と続いて、さすがに店員も苛ついてきた。しかし、とうとう完璧な帽子を見つけた父は、ニヤッと大きく微笑んで、母にそれを見せた。みんなホッと胸をなでおろしたが、それも母が帽子に目をやって、こう言うまでのことだった。「何言ってるのテッド、それ、あなたの帽子じゃない！」

　　　　　　　　　　　　　　　ジョーン・ウィルキンズ・ストーン
　　　　　　　　　　　　　　　ワシントン州ゴールデンデール

🎧098

BRONX CHEER

Al used to stand outside with his golf sweater on, always looking to play golf. So I went over and talked to him. He said, "Are you ready to play golf?" I said, "Not really. How about a game of ❶pool down in your ❷cellar?"

So that's what we did. We went downstairs and started to play on this big table that covered half the basement, but next to the pool table there happened to be a wood ❸column that supported the floors above. Every time I tried to use one of those long pool sticks, it would bump into the wood column.

🎧099

I said to Al, "I can't make this shot because of the column." Al said, "Why not cut the sticks?" I said, "That's a good idea," and so that's what I did.

Then I had a better idea. I said, "Al, maybe we should ❹eliminate this column and put a steel ❺beam in there instead." He said, "That's a great idea."

🎧100

So Al and I and the kids got into my station wagon and drove to 138th Street and Morris Avenue to pick up this twenty-two-foot steel beam for the house. The beam was so long that it stuck out of the station wagon. It kept hitting the street, ❻bouncing up and

---

(タイトル) Bronx Cheer: 本来は舌を震わせて出すあざけりの音のこと　❶pool: ビリヤード
❷cellar: 地下室、地階　❸column: 柱、支柱　❹eliminate: 〜を排除 [除去] する　❺beam: 梁
❻bounce: はねる

ブロンクス流どたばた

　アルはいつもゴルフセーターを着て、家の外に立ち、ゴルフに思いを馳せていた。で、僕は近寄っていって、話しかける。「ゴルフに行かないか」と彼。「ちょっとなあ。それより、君んちの地下室でビリヤードしようぜ」と僕。

　で、僕たちはそうする。階段を降りて、地下室の半分くらいある、でっかい玉突台でビリヤードをはじめた。でも、この玉突台の隣には、木の柱が居座っている。こいつで1階の床を支えてるわけだ。僕が長いキューを使おうとすると、きまってキューは柱にぶつかる。

　「柱が邪魔で打てないよ」

　「じゃあ、キューを削れば？」

　「そいつはいい考えだ」。で、僕はそうする。

　しばらくして、僕はもっといい考えを思いつく。「なあアル、この柱をとっぱらって、代わりに鉄の梁を入れればいいんじゃないかな」

　「そいつはいい考えだ」とアル。

　で、アルと僕と子供たちは、僕のステーションワゴンに乗って、138丁目とモリス・アベニューの角の店まで出かけ、7メートル近い鉄の梁を手に入れる。あんまり長いもんだから、梁はステーションワゴンからはみ出してしまう。道中ずっと、道路にぶつかり、ぴょんぴょん跳びは

down, and sparking and smoking. After a while the kids were yelling, "Hey, Daddy, look! The beam is on fire!"

🎧 101

Al and I both looked, and sure enough we had to stop and cool it off. Once we got into the house, we put the beam in the ❶driveway. Then we said, "How are we going to get this big beam into the house?"

I said that we had to cut a two-foot hole in the concrete wall. Then we'd be able to slide the beam under the ceiling of the basement.

So, we chopped the hole. I said to Al that before we put the steel beam in, we had to support the rest of the house with jacks and supporting wood columns. We didn't want the house to collapse before we took out the old wood column.

🎧 102

We worked until midnight. We were tired and ❷exhausted by then, so I went home. The next morning, around six o'clock, I got a call from Al. "Help!" he said. "I think there's something wrong. There's water coming down the steps, and the kids are yelling that they can't open the doors to the bathroom and the bedrooms to get out."

🎧 103

I ran across the street, and there's Al with his golf clubs and golf sweater, standing in front of the house and yelling at the kids,

---

❶driveway:（通りから建物・車庫までの）私道　❷exhausted: 疲れはてた

ね、火花を飛ばし、煙を上げる。すると、子供たちが叫んだ。「ねえ、お父さん、見て！　鉄が燃えてるよ」

　アルと僕が二人揃ってふり返ると、たしかに、車を停めて梁を冷やさなくちゃいけない事態になっている。家に戻るとすぐ、僕らは梁を玄関前の道に置く。「このでっかい梁、どうやって家のなかに入れようか？」

　コンクリートの壁に60センチほどの穴を空ければいい、と僕。そうすれば、地下室の天井の下に梁を滑り込ませることができる。

　で、僕たちは穴を空けた。僕はアルに言う。鉄の梁を運び込む前に、ほかのところをジャッキで支えて、木の柱の分を補強しないとね。古い柱をとっぱらう前に家の方が壊れるなんてごめんだからね。

　僕らは真夜中まで作業に取り組む。そのころにはくたくたに疲れきっている。で、僕は家に帰る。次の日の朝、6時ごろ、アルから電話がかかってくる。「助けてくれ！」と彼。「何か変なんだ。階段から水は落ちてくるし、子供たちはぎゃあぎゃあわめいてる。ドアが開かなくて、風呂場からも寝室からも出られないらしいんだ」

　僕は走って、通りを渡る。すると、アルがゴルフクラブとゴルフセーターを持って家の前に立ち、子供たちにどなっている。「水を止めろ！

"Turn off the water! Don't ❶flush the toilet! Your mother's downstairs on the table holding up the chandelier and ceiling with her hands!"

🎧 104

❷Sure enough, when I went into the house, that's exactly what I saw. Arlene was up there on the table, trying to keep the chandelier and ceiling from falling down. Al then ran upstairs and opened the doors for the kids to let them out. I ran downstairs into the basement and shut off the water. When I turned around, I saw ❸squirrels jumping in through the hole we had cut in the wall. The short, cut-down sticks were still on the table, and it looked like they were playing pool with them.

🎧 105

When I got upstairs, my wife was there, yelling at me that it was our anniversary. We have reservations in Canada, she says, did I forget? Hurry, hurry, we have to go.

I looked at Al and then at Arlene, who was ❹sopping wet, and at Al Jr. sliding down the ❺banister, and at Keith coming down the steps backwards on his knees, and he was sopping wet, too. Upstairs, the girls were yelling "Where's my clothes! My clothes are all wet!"

🎧 106

So I yelled out at the top of my voice, "STOP! Let's get Arlene off the table, and let's try to clean up this ❻mess so Al can go and

---

❶flush: (トイレなど) の水を流す ❷sure enough: はたして、案の定 ❸squirrel: リス ❹sopping wet: びしょ濡れになって ❺banister: (階段の) 手すり ❻mess: めちゃくちゃな様子、混乱

トイレを流すな！　母さんが1階で、テーブルの上に乗ってシャンデリアと天井を両手で支えてるんだぞ！」

　家のなかに入ると、たしかにその通りの光景が飛び込んできた。アーリーンがテーブルに乗って、シャンデリアと天井が落ちてこないようがんばっている。それから、アルが2階に駆け上がり、ドアを開けて子供たちを外に出してやる。僕は地下に駆け降りて、水を止める。ふり向くと、僕らが壁に空けた穴からリスたちが飛び込んでくるのが目に入る。短く削ったキューが何本かまだ玉突台の上にあって、リスたちがビリヤードしているみたいに見える。

　1階に上がると、僕の奥さんがいて、こっちに向かって叫んでいる。今日は私たちの結婚記念日なのよ。カナダのホテルに予約してあるの、忘れたの？　急いで、急いで、もう行かなくちゃ。

　僕はアルを見る。次に、びしょ濡れになったアーリーンと、手すりを滑って降りてくるアル・ジュニア、それから、やっぱりびしょ濡れになりながら、膝をついてうしろ向きにハイハイして階段を降りてくるキースを見る。2階では女の子たちが叫んでいる。「私の服はどこ？　ここにあるの全部びしょ濡れじゃない！」

　で、僕はあらんかぎりの声で叫ぶ。「ストップ！　アーリーンをテーブルから降ろすんだ。このしっちゃかめっちゃかを片づけて、アルがゴ

play golf."

I said to him, "I have to go on my anniversary trip, but when I come back, I'll try to put everything together again."

🎧 107

When I did come back, of course, Arlene had already put some ❶Sheetrock on the ceiling. She asked me to ❷plaster it and then paint the rest of the house, and that's what I did. But I still wanted to know what had happened, and Al said to me, "Just before you came that day, I had a carpenter come in to ❸shave and cut the doors to fit the ❹sagging house." I hadn't known about this so, quite naturally, when we ❺leveled off the house with our jacks and supports, we ❻straightened it out, and that's why nobody could open the doors.

🎧 108

You have to understand that this was not a normal house. It looked like something from that old comic book ❼*The Old Lady That Lived in a Shoe*, with forty kids looking out the windows. But, of course, that didn't ❽bother Al. He would say to Arlene, "Don't forget to plaster and paint the walls. And don't forget to pick out the color and ❾feed the kids before bedtime. I'm going to play golf." She would say, "Okay," but somehow, whenever she said okay, ❿out popped another kid. There were kids all over the place.

Joe Rizzo

Bronx, New York

---

❶Sheetrock: (商標) シートロック (紙のあいだに石膏を入れた建築用石膏ボード) ❷plaster: 〜にしっくいを塗る ❸shave: 〜の表面を削る、かんなをかける ❹sag: 傾く、ゆがむ ❺level off . . . : 〜を水平にする ❻straighten out . . . : 〜を真っすぐにする ❼*The Old Lady That Lived in a Shoe*: マザーグースの一節 "There was an old woman who lived in a shoe" に基づいた漫画 ❽bother: 〜を悩ます ❾feed: 〜に食べ物を与える ❿pop out: ひょっこり現われる (ここでは主語の another kid と述語の popped out が倒置され、さらに popped と out が倒置されている)

ルフに行けるようにしよう」

　僕はアルに言う。「僕は結婚記念の旅行に出かけなくちゃいけないけど、戻ってきたら、また元通りになるよう手伝うからね」

　もちろん僕は戻ってくる。すると、もうすでに天井にはアーリーンによって石膏ボードがはめられたあとだ。そいつにしっくいを塗って家の残りにもペンキを塗ってほしい、と彼女に頼まれる。で、僕はそうする。でも、まだ僕は事の真相を聞かされていない。アルが言う。「あの日、君が来るほんの少し前に、大工を呼んで、傾いた家に合わせてドアを削ってもらったんだよ」。僕はこのことを知らなかったわけで、至極当然の結果として、僕らがジャッキやら何やらで家を補強したことで家がまっすぐになってドアが開かなくなったというわけだ。

　はっきりさせておきたいんだが、こいつは普通の家じゃない。まるで、昔の漫画の『靴の中に住んでいたおばさん』にあった、40人の子供たちが窓から外をのぞいてるような家なんだ。でも、もちろん、アルは気にしちゃいない。彼はいつもアーリーンに言っている。「壁にしっくいとペンキを塗るのを忘れないようにな。それから、色をしっかり選ぶのと、寝る前に子供たちに食べさせるのも。俺はゴルフに行くから」。彼女は決まってこう言う。「わかったわ」。でも、どういうわけだか、彼女がわかったと言うたびに、またもう一人子供がひょっこり現われる。ここにはそこらじゅうに子供がいるのだ。

ジョー・リゾ
ニューヨーク州ブロンクス

🎧 109-151

STRANGERS

見知らぬ隣人

🎧 110

DANCING ON SEVENTY-FOURTH STREET
Manhattan, August 1962

A hot afternoon, my third day here. The studio apartment is ❶scorching. With a hammer and screwdriver I ❷chisel paint from the only window. Then, with one great ❸shove, I push the ❹jamb to the top and turn my head toward the unbroken line of ❺brownstones.

🎧 111

Next door, neighbors are ❻fanning out to the ❼stoops, where a brown-skinned infant ❽curls its lip and ❾arches its back before mama offers her nipple. In turquoise pants and clear plastic pumps, she sits cross-legged, ❿dangling her shoe from her toes, a newspaper between her and the hot ⓫cracking cement. While the newborn draws its milk, mama ⓬alternates between a thin cigar and a bottle of ⓭cerveza.

🎧 112

Papa in his undershirt ⓮swaggers out with a radio in one hand and a toddler dragging a broom in the other. The ⓯tot begins sweeping the stoop but changes its mind and ⓰strums the ⓱bristles instead. Kitchen chairs are being carried out, along with six-packs of ⓲Tab, 7Up and Rheingold.

※トラック109をはじめ、オースターによる導入のナレーションのスクリプトは、232〜235ページにまとめて掲載されています。
❶scorching: 焼けつくように暑い　❷chisel: 〜を彫る、削る　❸shove: 一押し、突くこと　❹jamb: (ドア・窓の) 脇柱　❺brownstone: ブラウンストーン (ニューヨークの古い建物の典型的な建築材料)　❻fan out: 四方に広がる　❼stoop: 玄関前の階段　❽curl one's lip: 口を歪める　❾arch: 〜を弓形に曲げる　❿dangle: 〜をぶら下げる　⓫cracking: ひび割れた　⓬alternate

74丁目のダンス
── 1962年8月、マンハッタン ──

　引っ越してきて3日目の、うだるような夕方。ワンルームのアパートは、まるで蒸し風呂だ。私はドライバーと金づちを使って、一つしかない窓枠にへばりついているペンキを削る。一気にぐいっと窓を押し上げると、頭を突き出して、どこまでも続くブラウンストーンの壁を左右に見渡す。

　すぐ隣の階段口に、アパートの住民たちが三々五々、出てきはじめている。階段には茶色い肌の赤ん坊を抱いたお母さんが座っていて、赤ん坊が口を歪め、体を弓なりにそらして泣きだすと、その口にお乳を含ませる。トルコブルーのズボンに透明ビニールのパンプスをはいたお母さんは、火傷しそうに熱いひび割れたコンクリートに新聞紙を敷いた上に足を組んで座り、つま先から一方の靴をぶらぶらさせている。赤ん坊をおっぱいに吸いつかせながら、細いシガーとビールの瓶を交互に口に運んでいる。

　そこにランニング姿のお父さんが、悠然と現れる。片手にラジオを下げ、もういっぽうの手には、ホウキをひきずった2、3歳の子供を連れている。子供は階段を掃こうとするが、途中で気が変わって、ギターを弾く真似をはじめる。あっちでもこっちでもキッチンから椅子が持ち出され、〈タブ〉や〈セブンナップ〉や〈ラインゴールド〉の6缶パックが運び出される。

---

between A and B: A と B のあいだを行きつ戻りつする　⓭cerveza:（スペイン語）ビール　⓮swagger: ふんぞり返って歩く　⓯tot: 赤ちゃん　⓰strum:（弦楽器・旋律）をかき鳴らす　⓱bristle:（ブラシなどの）毛（ここでは、ほうきの毛の部分を弾いて、ギターを弾くまねをしている）　⓲Tab, 7Up and Rheingold:タブとセブンナップは清涼飲料水、ラインゴールドはビール

🎧 113

I'm getting a ❶whiff of black beans and saffron rice steaming from the ❷hibachi under the stairs. Mama ties back her ❸brash red hair, ❹plops the baby in a box from Gristedes Market, and slowly begins to ❺twirl, her hands on her waist. She stops, ❻slinks over to her man, and, with her knee, ❼nudges his thigh. ❽Grinding to the sounds of the Caribbean, the pair ❾dodge, ❿plunge, twist, and ⓫swerve. The child ⓬accompanies with a wooden bowl and spoon; his father smiles in approval—flashing a gold ⓭incisor. Bongo players expand along the pavement while the new one sleeps in a cardboard box.

And I, a girl of twenty, a year out of Nebraska, watch ⓮transfixed. Suddenly, papa with the flashing incisor looks up from the ⓯pandemonium to my window.

"Hey ⓰muchacha!" he yells to me. "You got a smoke?"

Catherine Austin Alexander
Seattle, Washington

---

❶whiff: ほのかな香り　❷hibachi: ヒバチ (脚つきの鉄製バーベキューコンロ。日本語の「火鉢」から)　❸brash:(色が)派手な　❹plop: 〜をドサッと落とす　❺twirl: くるくる回る　❻slink: こっそり歩いていく　❼nudge: 〜をひじで軽く押す　❽grind:(挑発的に)腰を回す　❾dodge: 素早く身をよじる　❿plunge: 前のめりになる　⓫swerve: 急に向きを変える　⓬accompany: 伴奏する　⓭incisor: 切歯、門歯　⓮transfix: 〜を立ちすくませる　⓯pandemonium: 大混乱　⓰muchacha: (スペイン語)お嬢さん

階段の下に置かれた火鉢(ひばち)から、黒インゲンとサフランライスの匂いが、ぷんとここまで上がってくる。お母さんは、目の覚めるように赤い髪を一つにゆわえ、「グリスティーディス・マーケット」と書かれた段ボール箱のなかに赤ん坊を寝かしつけると、両手を腰に当てて、ゆっくりと円を描くように踊りはじめる。それからふと踊りやめ、連れ合いのところにそっと近づいていって、太腿を膝で軽く押す。ラジオのカリブ音楽のリズムに合わせ、二人は体をゆらし、くねらせ、跳ね、踊る。子供が木のボウルとスプーンで伴奏する。お父さんが、やるな、という顔でにっこり笑うと、のぞいた金の門歯がぴかりと光る。やがて歩道はボンゴを持った人々であふれ、それでも段ボールの中の赤ん坊はすやすやと眠っている。

　その光景を、ネブラスカから出てきて1年、まだ20歳の私は、あっけに取られて眺めている。すると下のお祭り騒ぎのなかから、さっきのピカピカ金歯のお父さんがひょいと顔をあげ、私に向かってこう叫ぶ。

「よう、姐(ムチャチャ)ちゃん！　タバコ、持ってないかい？」

キャサリン・オースティン・アレグザンダー

ワシントン州シアトル

🎧115

A SHOT IN THE LIGHT

Summer 1978: I was traveling through the Southwest as a jewelry and giftware salesman, selling a wide range of items from Austrian crystals to feather earrings. On the way to Los Angeles from Las Vegas, I stopped to help a motorist whose car had broken down in ❶the Mojave Desert. He was ❷down on his luck, had no plans and nowhere to go, so I let him travel with me.

🎧116

His name was Ray, and he looked to be in his early twenties. He was small, ❸muscular, ❹wiry, and slightly ❺gaunt, as if ❻underfed. I felt sorry for him, and in the three days we were together, I grew to trust him. I even started ❼sending him on errands while I visited stores to sell my wares. At one point, I gave him some of my clothes, and it pleased him to have something new to wear. He seemed calm and mostly satisfied.

🎧117

The third night, we were ❽camped out near Puddingstone ❾Reservoir east of ❿Claremont. I was sitting on the floor in the back of the large van, moving things around in the cupboards to make more room for the clothes, books, food, sample boxes, and my passenger's ⓫duffel bag and travel gear.

（タイトル）A shot in the light: "a shot in the dark"（闇の中の一撃、あてずっぽう）をふまえた言い方　❶the Mojave Desert: モハーヴィ砂漠（カリフォルニア州南部の砂漠）　❷down on one's luck: つきに見放されて、落ちぶれて　❸muscular: 筋肉質の　❹wiry: 痩せ型の　❺gaunt: 痩せこけた、やつれた　❻underfed: 栄養不良の　❼send ... on an errand: 〜を使いにやる　❽camp out: 野宿する　❾reservoir: 貯水池　❿Claremont: クレアモント（カリフォルニア州南西部の町）　⓫duffel bag: 雑嚢、ダッフルバッグ（ズック製の円筒形の袋。元は軍人が用いた）

怪我の「光明」

　1978年の夏。アクセサリーとギフト用品のセールスマンをしていた私は、南西部を旅しながら、オーストリア産水晶から羽根のイヤリングまで手広く売り歩いていた。ラスヴェガスからロサンゼルスに向かう途中、モハーヴィ砂漠で車がエンストして困っていた旅行者を助けた。聞けば無一文で、行くあても先の見通しもないというので、一緒に連れていってやることにした。

　レイという名前で、年格好は20代前半といったところだった。背は低く、痩せているが筋肉質で、ただあまりまともに食べていないのか、少しやつれた感じに見えた。私はレイを気の毒に思い、3日間一緒に過ごすうちに、だんだん気を許すようになった。自分が商店に品物を売りに行っている間に、ちょっとした用事を頼んだりもした。ある時、私が服を少しあげると、新しい服が着られると言って喜んでいた。いかにも穏やかそうで、これといって不満を抱いているようにも見えなかった。

　3日目の夜は、クレアモントの東にあるパディングストン貯水池のそばでキャンプした。そのとき私は大型バンの後部の床に座りこみ、戸棚の中に入っている物を入れなおして、衣類や本、食料、サンプルの箱、レイのダッフルバッグや旅行道具などが入るようにしていた。

🎧 **118**

There was a loud explosion, and I felt a sharp, ❶searing blow to the top of my head. Had the gas stove exploded? I looked up, but it was ❷intact. Then I looked at Ray sitting in the driver's seat, and I saw the black gun in his hand. His arm was resting on the back of the seat, aiming the pistol at my face. A bullet had hit me! At first, I thought he was warning me—that he was going to rob me. That suddenly seemed fine. Take it all, I thought. Take it all. Just leave me outside and drive away.

🎧 **119**

Another explosion shook me, and my ears rang with a terrible, high-pitched ❸whine. I felt blood dripping down my face, and the top of my head ❹throbbed. He's not warning me, I realized. He's going to kill me. I am going to die.

🎧 **120**

There was no place to hide. I was stuck in an uncomfortable position surrounded by cabinets. There was nothing I could do. I heard myself whisper, "Relax. It's out of your control. Breathe. Stay awake." My thoughts turned to death, and to God. "❺Thy will, not my will, be done." I let my body go, and I started to relax, to ❻slump back. I watched my breath, in and out, in and out, in and out. . . .

🎧 **121**

I began preparing for my death. I asked to be forgiven by anyone

---

❶searing: 燃えるような、焼けつくような　❷intact: 損なわれていない、傷ついていない　❸whine: 甲高い音　❹throb:（痛みなどで）ずきずきする　❺Thy will be done.: 御心が行われますように。(『聖書』マタイによる福音書、6：10)　❻slump: どさりと座り込む

ふいに大きな破裂音がして、頭のてっぺんに焼けつくような鋭い衝撃を感じた。ガスレンジが爆発したのか？　そっちの方を見たが、レンジに異状はなかった。それからレイを見ると、運転席に座って、手に黒い銃を握りしめていた。腕をシートの背にのせ、銃をまっすぐ私の顔に向けている。では今のは銃弾だったのだ！　はじめは脅しているのだと思った――脅して、金品を奪おうとしているのだ、と。それなら構わないと、なぜか突然思った。全部持っていくがいい。俺を外に放り出して、車ごと持っていくといい。

　また破裂音がして激しい衝撃を感じ、キーンとつんざくような音が耳の中で鳴り響いた。顔を血が伝い落ち、頭のてっぺんがずきずきした。これは脅しじゃない、と私は気づいた。殺す気なんだ。俺は死ぬんだ。

　身を隠せる場所はどこにもなかった。棚と棚の間にはさまれた窮屈な姿勢のまま、身動きが取れなかった。万事休すだ。自然に言葉が口からもれた――「落ち着け。じたばたしたって始まらない。息をしろ。目を閉じるな」。私の心はしだいに死を、神を、思いはじめた。「神よ、私のではなく、あなたの御心をなしたまえ」。体から力が抜け、戸棚にぐったりもたれかかった。自分の呼吸にじっと神経を集中させた――吸って、吐いて、吸って、吐いて、吸って、吐いて……。

　私は死に向かいはじめていた。今までに傷つけてしまったすべての人

I had hurt and offered my forgiveness to everyone who had hurt me throughout my life. It was a full-color fast-reverse movie reel of my entire twenty-six years. I thought about my parents, my brothers and sisters, my lovers, my friends. I said good-bye. I said, "I love you."

🎧 122

Another explosion shook the van, and my body pulsed. I was not hit. The bullet missed me by a ❶fraction of an inch, ❷penetrating the cupboard I was leaning against. I relaxed back into my ❸reverie. My luck could not ❹hold out. Three bullets to go, if it was a revolver. I could only hope that the gun wasn't a ❺semiautomatic.

🎧 123

Nothing mattered anymore but to be at peace. My van, my money, my business, my knowledge, my personal history, my freedom—all became worthless, meaningless, ❻so much dust in the wind.

All I had of value was my body and my life, and that was soon to be gone. My attention was focused on the spark of light I called my Self, and my consciousness began to expand outward, extending my awareness in space and time. I heard my instructions clearly: STAY AWAKE AND KEEP BREATHING.

🎧 124

I prayed to my God, to the Great Spirit, to receive me with open arms. Love and light flowed through me, spreading out like a lighthouse beam, illuminating everything around me. The light grew in-

---

❶ fraction: 何分の一　❷ penetrate:（弾丸などが）〜を貫く　❸ reverie: 夢想、空想　❹ hold out: もつ、続く　❺ semiautomatic: セミ＝オートマチック、半自動小銃　❻ so much dust: それだけの量の土埃（「きわめて多量の〜」ではない）

に赦しを乞い、今までに自分を傷つけたすべての人を赦す気になった。まるで総天然色の映画フィルムを高速で巻き戻すように、26年間の自分の全人生が見えた。両親やきょうだい、恋人、友人たちの顔が、つぎつぎ脳裡に浮かんだ。その一人ひとりに、私はさようならを言った。「愛しているよ」そう言った。

　また破裂音がバン全体に響きわたり、体がびくんと動いた。弾は当たらなかった。私の体をぎりぎりかすめ、もたれかかっている戸棚に穴を開けた。私はふたたび力を抜き、夢想の世界に入っていった。幸運はそう何度も続くまい。あの銃がリボルバーだとしても、弾はあと3発あるはずだ。せめてセミ＝オートマチックでないことを祈るしかない。

　ただひたすら心安らかになりたい。他のことはどうでもよかった。バンも、金も、仕事も、知識も、これまでの人生も、自由も ―― すべてが風に舞う土埃のように、無価値で無意味なものに思えた。

　唯一価値あるものはこの肉体と命だけだったが、それもじきに消え去る運命だ。私の心の眼は、私が自分で〈ワタシ〉と呼んでいる、ちかちかとまたたく光に向けられていた。意識がしだいに外へ向かって拡大していき、時間・空間の感覚が大きく広がった。さっき自分に言い聞かせた言葉が、はっきりと聞こえた ――「**目を閉じるな、息をしろ**」。

　私は神と精霊とに、どうかその両腕で受け止めてくださいと祈った。愛と光が体じゅうに満ち、灯台の光のように外に向かってあふれだし、周囲のものすべてを明るく照らした。体内の光はしだいに強さを増して

side me, and I expanded like a huge balloon until the van and its contents seemed small. A sense of peace and acceptance filled me. I knew I was close to leaving my body. I could sense the timeline of my life, both backward and forward. I saw the next bullet, a short distance into the future, leave the gun, jet toward my left temple, and exit with brains and blood on the right side of my head. I was filled with awe. To see life from this expanded ❶perspective was like looking down into a dollhouse, seeing all the rooms at once, all the detail, so real and so unreal at the same time. I looked into the warm and welcoming golden light with calm and acceptance.

🎧 125

The fourth explosion ❷shattered the silence, and my head was pushed violently to the side. The ringing in my ears was ❸deafening. Warm blood rushed down my head and onto my arms and thighs, dripping onto the floor. But strangely, I found myself back in my body, not out of it. Still surrounded by light, love, and peace, I began looking inside my skull, trying to find the holes. Perhaps I could see light through them? I did a quick check of my feelings, abilities, thoughts, and sensations, looking for what might be missing. Surely the bullet had affected me. My head was throbbing, but I felt strangely normal.

🎧 126

I decided to look at my ❹assassin, to look death in the face. I picked up my head and turned my eyes toward him. He was

---

❶ perspective: 視点、見通し　❷ shatter: 〜を粉々にする　❸ deafening: 耳をつんざくような　❹ assassin: 暗殺者、刺客

いき、私はまるで風船のように大きく大きくふくらんで、バンもその中身もちっぽけに見えた。安らかな諦念が私を満たしていった。もうすぐこの肉体を離れるのだということが、はっきりとわかった。自分の人生が一つの年表のように見え、過去も、未来も、同時に見ることができた。ごくごく近い将来に発射されるであろう次の銃弾も見えた。それはピストルを離れ、私の左のこめかみに向かって飛んできて、脳味噌や血と一緒に頭の右側から出てくるはずだった。私は言い知れぬ思いに圧倒された。はるか上の視点から自分の人生を見下ろしていると、まるでドールハウスを真上から覗き込んでいるように、すべての部屋や、その中のこまごまとしたものまでが一度に見えた。それはとてもリアルでありながら、同時にひどく非現実的な感覚だった。私は静かな、澄みきった気持ちで、あたたかく誘いかけてくるような黄金の光と向き合っていた。

　4度目の破裂音が静けさを打ち破り、頭ががくんと片側にかしいだ。耳の中で、耐えがたいほど大きな音がガンガン鳴り響いた。頭から生温かい血が勢いよく噴き出し、腕や腿を濡らし、床にもぼたぼた垂れた。だが不思議なことに、私の魂はふたたび体の中に引き戻されていた。光と愛と安息に包まれたまま、私は自分の頭蓋骨の内側に目を向け、穴の開いている箇所を探した。もしかしたら、その部分から光が洩れてきているかもしれないと思った。自分の感情、体の機能、気分、感覚を素早く点検し、何か欠落したものはないかチェックした。弾丸は私の体にダメージを与えた、それは間違いなかった。頭がずきずき痛んだ。が、不思議なくらい平常心だった。

　私は意を決して、自分を殺そうとしている者の顔を —— 死神の顔を —— この目で見ることにした。頭を持ち上げ、目を彼のほうに向けた。

shocked. Jumping up from his seat, he shouted, "Why aren't you dead, man? You're supposed to be dead!"

"Here I am," I said quietly.

"That's too ❶weird! It's just like my dream this morning! I kept shooting at him, but he wouldn't die! But it wasn't you in the dream, it was somebody else!"

🎧 127

This was very strange. Who was writing the script? I wondered. I began to speak slowly and calmly, trying to settle him down. If I could get him talking, I thought, maybe he wouldn't shoot again. He kept yelling, "Shut up! Just shut up!" as he ❷peered out the windows into the darkness. He nervously walked closer to me, gun in hand, examining my bloody head, trying to understand why the four bullets he had ❸pumped into me hadn't finished me off.

🎧 128

I could still feel blood ❹oozing down my face and could hear it dripping onto my shoulder. Ray said, "I don't know why you aren't dead, man. I shot you four times!"

"Maybe I'm not supposed to die," I said calmly.

"Yeah, but I shot you!" he said, with disappointment and confusion in his voice. "I don't know what to do."

"What do you want to do?" I asked.

"I wanted to kill you, man, to take this van and drive away. Now I don't know." He seemed worried, uncertain. He was beginning to

---

❶weird: 不可解な、気味悪い　❷peer: じっと見る　❸pump: (銃弾)を浴びせる　❹ooze: じくじくとしみ出る

彼はぎょっとなった。シートから後ずさり、悲鳴を上げた。「なんで生きてんだよ！　ふつう死ぬだろ？」
「死んでない」私は静かに言った。
「おっかねえ！　けさ見た夢そのまんまだ！　誰かに向かって何度も銃をぶっぱなすんだが、そいつ死なねえんだ！　でもあんたじゃなかった、別の奴だったのに！」
　妙なことになってきた。一体どっちが主導権を握っているんだ？　私は彼を落ち着かせようと、静かな口調でゆっくり話しだした。彼にしゃべらせておくかぎり、撃ってこないかもしれないと考えたのだ。だが彼は「うるせえ！　黙れ！」とわめき、窓の外の暗闇をすかして見た。それから銃を手にしたままそろそろと近づいてきて、血だらけの私の頭をしげしげ見つめた。4発も弾をぶちこんだのにどうして死なないのか、理解できないといった様子だった。
　血はあいかわらず顔を伝い落ち、肩にぽたぽた滴り落ちていた。レイは言った。「なんで死なねえんだよ。4発撃ったんだぜ！」
「きっとまだ死なない運命なんだろう」私は静かに言った。
「だって、ピストルで撃ったんだぜ！」彼は失望ととまどいのいりまじった声で言った。「どうすりゃいいんだ、俺」
「きみはどうしたいんだ？」私は訊いた。
「あんたを殺して、このバンで逃げようと思ってた。でも、もうどうすりゃいいのかわかんねえ」彼は不安げな、ためらうような表情を見せた。だいぶ落ち着いてきて、さっきまでの興奮状態はおさまってきてい

slow down, to become less ❶jumpy.

🎧129

"Why did you want to kill me?"

"Because you had everything, and I had nothing. And I was tired of having nothing. This was my chance to have it all." He was still pacing back and forth in the van, looking out the windows at the black night outside.

"What do you want to do now?" I asked.

"I don't know, man," he complained. "Maybe I should take you to the hospital."

🎧130

My heart leapt at this chance, this opportunity—a way out. "Okay," I said, not wanting to make him feel out of control. I wanted it to be his idea, not mine. I knew that his anger ❷sprang from feeling out of control, and I didn't want to make him feel angry.

"Why were you so nice to me, man?"

"Because you're a person, Ray."

"But I wanted to kill you! I kept taking out my gun and pointing it at you, when you were asleep or not looking. But you were being so nice to me, I couldn't do it."

🎧131

My time sense was altered. I realized that I had no idea how long it had been since the first bullet. After what felt like many minutes,

---

❶jumpy: びりびりした　❷spring from . . . :（感情などが）〜から生じる

るようだった。

「どうして俺を殺そうとした？」

「あんたが何もかも持ってて、俺は何も持ってないからさ。俺はもう無一文には飽き飽きなんだ。俺にとっちゃ、すべてを手に入れるチャンスだった」。彼はあいかわらずそわそわとバンの中を歩き回り、ときおり窓の外の暗闇に目をやった。

「で、今はどうしたい？」私はたずねた。

「わかんねえ」彼は苦しげに言った。「あんたを病院に連れてくべきなのかもしれない」

願ってもないチャンスに胸が高鳴った。もしかしたら助かるかもしれない。「なるほど」私に優位に立たれたと彼に感じさせないよう、控えめにそう言った。私からではなく、彼が自分から言い出すように仕向けたかった。彼の怒りは、自分が主導権を奪われているという思いから発していた。怒りをあおるようなことはしたくなかった。

「あんた、なんで俺にあんなに親切にしたんだ？」

「助け合うのが人間ってもんだろ」

「でも、俺はあんたを殺そうとしてたんだぜ！　あんたが寝てる時とか向こうを向いてる時とかに、何度も銃を出して狙ったんだ。でもあんたがあんまり親切にしてくれるもんだから、どうしても撃てなかった」

時間の感覚が狂いはじめていた。1発目の銃弾からどれくらい時が経ったのか、まるでわからなくなっていた。何十分にも思える時間が

Ray came up to me, still in my crouched, locked-in position, and said, "Okay, man, I'm going to take you to a hospital. But I don't want you to move, so I'm going to put some stuff on you so you can't move, okay?"

🎧132

Now he was asking my permission. "Okay," I said softly. He began taking various boxes filled with samples and stacked them around me. "Are you okay?" he asked.

"Yeah, I'm okay. A little uncomfortable, but it's all right."

"Okay, man. I'm going to take you to a hospital I know of. Now don't move. And don't ❶die on me, okay?"

"Okay," I promised. I knew I wouldn't die. This light, this power inside me was so strong, so certain. Each breath felt like my first, not my last. I was going to survive. I knew it. Ray lowered the ❷pop-top of the van, ❸secured the straps, and started up the engine. I could feel the van backing up on the dirt road, finding the pavement and moving forward to my freedom.

🎧133

He drove on and on—to where, I had no idea. Were we bound for a hospital, as he said, or toward some horrible fate? If he was capable of killing me with a gun, he was capable of lying, or worse. How did he know where to go? We were in Claremont. Los Angeles was over an hour away. I used that hour to replay the scenes and analyze the past three days, trying to understand what had hap-

---

❶die on . . . : 〜の目の前で死ぬ　❷pop-top: ポップアップ式の天井　❸secure: 〜をしっかり固定する

経ってから、レイが窮屈にうずくまったままの姿勢でいる私のところに近づいてきて、言った。「わかった。あんたを病院に連れてくよ。ただし動かれちゃ困るから、周りに物を置いて動けなくする。いいか？」

　いつの間にか、向こうがこっちに許可を求めていた。「ああ、いいよ」私は穏やかに言った。彼は商品サンプルの入ったいろいろな形の箱を持ってきて、それを私の周りに積み上げた。「大丈夫か？」

「ああ、大丈夫だ。ちょっと狭いが、問題ない」

「よし、じゃあこれから俺の知ってる病院に連れてくよ。ただし、動くなよ。それから、死ぬんじゃないぞ」

「ああ」私は約束した。まるで死ぬ気がしなかった。体に宿ったこの光、このパワーは、強力でゆるぎなかった。一つ呼吸をするたびに、死ぬどころか生まれ変わっていくような気がした。私はきっと助かる。レイは押し上げてあったバンのルーフを下ろし、ストラップを固定すると、エンジンをかけた。バンがでこぼこ道をバックし、舗道に出て、私の自由に向けて走りだすのがわかった。

　車はいつまでも走り続けた —— 私の知らないどこかへ向かって。私たちは本当に病院を目指しているのだろうか、それとも何か恐ろしい結末に向かっているのだろうか？　何といっても相手は私を撃ち殺そうとした人間だ。嘘をつくぐらいのことは平気でやりかねない。だいいち、本当に行くあてなどあるのだろうか？　ここはクレアモント、ロサンゼルスまでは1時間以上の道のりだ。私はその時間を利用して、この3日間のさまざまな場面を頭の中で再現し、分析し、いったい何が起こった

pened and why.

🎧 134

Eventually I felt the van slow, ❶pull over, and stop. The engine was turned off. Silence filled the space. I waited. It was still dark outside. We had not pulled into a ❷driveway. There were no lights. This was not a hospital.

🎧 135

Ray walked back toward me with his gun in his hand. He pulled away one of the boxes and sat down on the foam bed, facing me. He looked ❸distraught, head hanging down. His words cut deep through my cloud of hope. "I have to kill you, man," he said calmly.

"Why?" I asked quietly.

🎧 136

"If I take you to the hospital, they'll put me back in jail. I can't go back to jail, man. I can't."

"They wouldn't put you in jail if you take me to the hospital," I said slowly, still ❹feigning injury, ❺passivity. I knew that I might find an opening, a moment when I could surprise him, ❻overpower him, take away his gun. As long as he didn't know I was okay, I had an advantage.

"Oh yes they would, man. They'd know I shot you, and they'd lock me up."

"We don't have to tell them. I won't tell them."

---

❶pull over:（車が）（道の）片側に寄る　❷driveway:（通りから建物・車庫への）私道　❸distraught: 取り乱した、ろうばいした　❹feign: 〜を装う　❺passivity: 無抵抗、服従　❻overpower: 〜を（力で）圧倒する

のか、そしてなぜそれが起こったのかを理解しようとつとめた。

　やがてバンはスピードをゆるめ、路肩に寄って停まった。エンジンが切られた。静けさがあたりを包んだ。私はじっとしていた。外はあいかわらず真っ暗だった。どこかの敷地内に入ったという感じではなかった。明かりはどこにも見えなかった。どう考えても病院ではない。

　レイが銃を持って近づいてきた。箱を一つどけて、ウレタンのマットレスに腰を下ろし、私と向き合った。途方にくれた顔つきで、首を力なくうなだれていた。彼の口から出た言葉が、私の希望の雲を切り裂いた。「やっぱりあんたを殺さなきゃ」彼は落ち着いた声で言った。

　「なぜだ？」私は静かに訊き返した。

　「あんたを病院に連れてけば、俺はまた監獄に逆戻りだ。あそこにだけは戻りたくない。絶対に」

　「俺を病院に連れていってくれれば、監獄になんか入れられないさ」私はあくまで無力な怪我人のふりをして、のろのろと言った。いずれはきっかけが見つかるはずだった。その瞬間をとらえ、不意打ちをくらわせて、力ずくで銃を奪うのだ。彼が私のことを弱っていると思っているかぎり、分はこっちにある。

　「いいや、入れられるとも。俺が撃ったってことがわかれば、すぐに監獄に入れられちまう」

　「誰にも言わなければいい。俺は言わないよ」

🎧 **137**

"I can't trust you, man. I wish I could, but I can't. I can't go back to jail, that's all. I have to kill you." He seemed ❶forlorn. This was not where he wanted to be. He wasn't making any moves. His gun hung ❷limply from his hand, pointed down toward the floor. The boxes were still stacked around me. I couldn't judge how much strength I had, whether it would be enough to push out and wrestle him down. He was small but strong. Was he still full of adrenaline? That would make him even stronger. My strength lay in words, in verbal ❸swordplay. If I could keep him talking, he wouldn't take stronger action.

🎧 **138**

"Maybe I could go into the hospital alone, Ray. You wouldn't even have to be there. You could get away."

"No, man," he said, shaking his head. "As soon as you told them, they'd come find me. They'd ❹track me down."

I was silent. That didn't work, I thought.

🎧 **139**

He said, "Why aren't you dead, man? I shot you *four times* in the head. How come you're still alive and talking? You should be dead! I know I didn't miss." He looked again at my head, taking it in one hand and turning it to the left and right. "Does it hurt?" he asked. He seemed ❺genuinely concerned.

"Yeah, it hurts," I lied. "But I think I'm going to be okay."

---

❶forlorn: 希望を失った、絶望した　❷limply: 弱々しく　❸swordplay: 剣術、剣さばき　❹track...down: （犯人など）の居所をつきとめる　❺genuinely: 真に、本気で

「そんなの信じられるもんか。信じたいが、無理だ。ともかく、監獄にだけは戻りたくないんだ。だからあんたを殺すしかない」。彼は追い詰められたような目をしていた。こんなはずじゃなかったのに、と自分でも思っているのだろう。なかなか動こうとはしなかった。手をだらりと下げ、銃を床に向けていた。私の周りには、箱が積み上げられたままだった。ここから跳ね起きて彼を組み伏せるだけの体力が、まだ私に残っているだろうか。相手は小柄だが、力は強い。もしまだアドレナリンが引いていなかったら？　だとすれば、ますます危ない。やはり私には言葉しかない。言葉を武器に、この場を切り抜けるのだ。ずっと話させておけば、彼も荒っぽい手には出ないはずだ。
　「じゃあレイ、俺が一人で病院に行くよ。きみはついて来なくていい。一人で逃げろ」
　「駄目だ」レイは首を振った。「あんたが話したら、すぐに連中が追っかけてくる。そうなりゃいずれ捕まっちまう」
　私は黙った。これじゃ駄目だ。
　彼は言った。「あんた、ほんとになんで死なないんだよ？　4発も頭にくらってるんだぜ。どうして生きて、平気でしゃべってるんだ？　あんたは死んでなきゃいけないんだ！　俺はたしかに撃ったのに！」。彼は私の頭を片手でつかみ、右、左と動かしながらもう一度しげしげ眺めた。「痛いか？」本気で心配そうだった。
　「ああ、痛い」私は嘘をついた。「でも、たぶん大丈夫だ」

"Well, I don't know what to do. I can't take you to the hospital. I can't just let you go, because you'll call the police. Why were you so ❶damn nice to me, man? No one's ever been that nice to me before. It made it harder to kill you. You kept buying me stuff and giving me stuff. I just couldn't decide when to do it."

Not if, but when.

🎧 140

"What would you do with all this stuff if you had it, Ray?" I asked.

"I could go home and ❷be somebody, I could do stuff. I'd have enough money to buy my way out of there, man." Ray began to talk. He talked about his home in East Los Angeles, the poverty around him, his anger, the schoolteachers who made him feel stupid, his father who drank too much and beat him, and being tough on the streets. He talked about joining the army, how that was supposed to make it work, but he couldn't stand being told what to do all the time, so he went ❸AWOL. He talked about dealing drugs, and drug deals going bad, and how he ❹ripped off his dealer buddies. That's why he had to leave L.A., because they were looking for him. He talked about stealing his father's gun and money before he left, then he realized there was no place to hide, so he decided to turn back. Maybe he could do one more rip-off and get rich. He just needed one hit, one ❺sucker. If his target was rich enough, he could ❻pay off the dealers and start over. So he decided to kill who-

---

❶damn: とても、ひどく　❷be somebody: いっぱしの人間になる、一旗あげる　❸AWOL: 無断[無許可]離隊の（Absence Without Leave）　❹rip off ...: 〜から金をだまし取る（5行下では名詞として使われている）　❺sucker: カモ　❻pay off ...: 〜に借りをすっかり返す

「俺、一体どうしたらいいんだ。あんたを病院に連れてくわけにはいかない。でも一人で行かせるわけにもいかない、警察に言うにきまってるからな。あんた、どうしてあんなに優しくなんかしやがったんだよ？今まで誰もこんなに優しくなんかしてくれなかったのに。おかげでどうしても殺せなかった。しょっちゅう物をくれたり、買ってくれたりするもんだから、いつ殺ればいいのか、決心がつけられなかった」

　殺るか殺らないか、ではない。いつ殺るか、なのだ。

「もしここにあるものが全部手に入ったら、どうする気だ？」私はたずねた。

「故郷に帰って、一旗あげるのさ。これだけあれば何だってできる。金を貯めて、あそこの暮らしから抜け出すんだ」。レイは語りはじめた。生まれ育ったイースト・ロサンゼルスのこと。そこでの貧しさ。彼の怒り。彼を馬鹿にした学校の教師たちのこと。酔っては彼を殴る父親のこと。街で不良の仲間入りをしたこと。出直そうと軍隊に入ったが、いちいち人から命令されるのに耐えられず、無許可離隊してしまったこと。それからドラッグの売人になったが、商売がうまくいかなくなり、売人仲間から金をだまし取ったこと。追われる身になって、LAを出ていかなければならなくなったこと。父親のピストルと金を盗んで出てきたが、結局どこにも行き場がなく、引き返すことにした。もう一度誰かから金をとれば、うまくいくかもしれない。あともう一回、あともう一人だけ。もしも運よく金持ちに当たれば、その金で売人仲間に借りを返して、また一からやり直せる。だから誰でもいい、最初に車を停めた人間

ever stopped. Whoever came by to help him. Me.

🎧 141

The night had turned to morning, the sky shifting slowly from ❶indigo to blue. The sound of ❷chirping birds made me grateful to be alive.

"I'm pretty ❸stiff and ❹sore, Ray. I'd feel better if I could get up and stretch." I was still in the same position I had been in for six hours. Dried blood was ❺plastered to my hair and face, my ❻shins hurt from being pushed against the edge of a cupboard door, and my back was stiff and ❼throbbing.

"Okay, man, I'm going to let you get up, but don't do anything stupid, okay?"

"Okay, Ray. You just tell me what to do and I'll do it."

Remind him that he is in control. Don't let him feel out of control. Look for an opening.

🎧 142

He moved the boxes from around me, stepped back with the gun in his hand, and opened the door. I ❽crawled slowly out of the van, stretching upright for the first time. How beautiful the world was to my new eyes. Everything shone as if made of sparkling crystal.

🎧 143

We had stopped on a ❾residential street near a small pond at the bottom of an ❿embankment. He gestured down the dirt trail that led to the water. As I walked down the steep ⓫incline I thought, "Is

---

❶indigo: (濃い) 藍色　❷chirp: (鳥が) チュンチュンと鳴く　❸stiff: (体・筋肉などが) 硬くなってうまく動かない　❹sore: (体が) 痛い、ヒリヒリする　❺plaster: 〜をべたべた塗る　❻shin: 向こうずね　❼throb: ずきずきする　❽crawl: 這って行く　❾residential street: 住宅地　❿embankment: (道路などの) 土手　⓫incline: 傾斜面

を殺そうと決めた。彼を助けるために車を停めた人間を。それが私だった。

　夜はいつしか朝になり、空がゆっくり藍色から青に変わりはじめていた。鳥のさえずりが聞こえ、私はまだ生きていることの有り難みを噛みしめた。

　「なあレイ、足腰が痛くなってきた。立ち上がって、体を伸ばしたいんだがな」。もう6時間も同じ姿勢のままだった。乾いた血が髪や顔にこびりつき、脛はずっと戸棚の縁に押しつけられて痛み、背中は凝ってずきずきした。

　「オーケー、いま立たせてやる。ただし、妙な気を起こすんじゃないぞ」

　「わかった。全部きみに言われた通りにするよ」

　あくまで彼が主導権を握っていると思わせておく必要がある。ちょっとでも優位に立たれたと感じさせてはならない。今はただきっかけを待つのだ。

　彼は私の周りの箱をどけると、銃を構えて一歩下がり、ドアを開けた。私はゆっくりとバンの外に這い出て、実に久しぶりに立って体を伸ばした。生まれ変わった私の目に、世界はたとえようもなく美しく映った。あらゆるものがキラキラと、まるできらめくクリスタルでできているように輝いた。

　バンが停まっていたのは住宅の並ぶ一角で、そのすぐそば、道路脇の土手を下ったところに、小さな池があった。池に降りる舗装していない小道を歩いていくよう、レイは私に身振りで示した。急な坂を下りなが

this death again, tapping on my shoulder? Will he shoot me in the back and push me into the water?" I felt weak and ❶vulnerable, yet simultaneously ❷immortal and ❸impervious to his bullets. I walked erect and unafraid. He followed me to the water's edge and stood by as I squatted down and rinsed my bloodied hands and face, splashing cool, fresh water on myself. I stood up slowly and faced Ray. He looked at me curiously.

🎧 144

"What would you do if I handed you this gun right now?" he asked, holding the gun out to me.

My answer was my first thought: "I'd throw it out into the water," I said.

"Aren't you mad at me, man?" he asked. He seemed ❹incredulous.

"No, why should I be mad?"

"I shot you, man, you ought to be angry! I'd be ❺fucking ❻furious! You wouldn't want to kill me if I gave you this gun?"

"No, Ray, I wouldn't. Why should I? I have my life and you have yours."

🎧 145

"I don't understand you, man. You are really weird, really different than anyone I've ever met before. And I don't know why you didn't die when I shot you." Silence. Better left unanswered. As we stood at the water's edge, I realized that Ray had ❼undergone a

---

❶vulnerable: 傷つきやすい、もろい　❷immortal: 不死身の　❸impervious to ...: 〜を受けつけない　❹incredulous: 信じられないという様子で　❺fucking: ひどく　❻furious: 怒り狂った　❼undergo: 〜を経験する

ら、私は思った——「またしても死神が俺の肩を叩いているんだろうか？　俺を背後から撃って、池に放り込む気だろうか？」。私は気が弱って今にも倒れそうだったが、同時に自分は不死身だ、銃弾にも倒れない、と感じていた。胸を張って堂々と歩いた。彼は私の後について水際まで行き、私がしゃがんで血まみれの顔と手を洗い、ひんやり心地よい水をぱしゃぱしゃ顔にかけるのを、横に立ってじっと見ていた。私はゆっくり立ち上がり、レイと向き合った。彼は不思議なものを見る目つきで私を見た。

「もしも俺が今この銃を渡したら、あんたどうする？」彼は私に銃を差し出し、そう訊いた。

私は思ったままを答えた。「池に捨てるね」

「俺のこと、怒っていないのか？」彼は訊いた。信じられないという顔をしていた。

「いいや。なんで怒らなくちゃならないんだ」

「だって俺はあんたを撃ったんだぜ。ふつう怒るだろ！　俺だったらメチャクチャ怒るぜ！　この銃を渡されても、俺を撃ちたいと思わないのか？」

「いいや、思わないね。思うわけないじゃないか。俺の命は俺のものだし、きみの命はきみのものだ」

「わかんねえよ。あんた変だよ。こんな変わった奴、見たことがない。だいいち撃たれたのに死なないなんて、どうかしてるよ」。沈黙。ここは黙っていたほうがいいだろう。二人並んで水辺に立っていると、レイ

❶transformation as deep as the one I had. We were no longer the same people we had been the day before.

🎧 146

"What should we do now, Ray?"

"I don't know, man. I can't take you to the hospital. I can't let you go. I don't know what to do."

🎧 147

So we continued our talk, seeking a solution to his dilemma. We explored the possibilities—what could we agree to? I made suggestions, he told me why they wouldn't work. I made other suggestions. He listened, considered, rejected, and ❷relented. We sought a ❸compromise.

🎧 148

Ultimately, we found a bargain we could agree on: I would let him go, and he would let me go. I promised not to ❹turn him in or report him to the police, but on one condition—he had to promise that he would *never* do anything like this again. He promised. What choice did he have?

🎧 149

As the sun was rising over the hills, we climbed back into the van. I sat in the passenger seat as he drove to a place that he knew. He parked, and I gave him all the cash I had, about two hundred dollars, and a couple of watches I thought he could ❺pawn. We walked together across the street. The sun was shining. It was early

---

❶transformation: 変化、変容　❷relent: 気持ちを和らげる　❸compromise: 妥協点　❹turn . . . in: (容疑者など)を引き渡す、密告する　❺pawn: 〜を質に入れる

もまた私と同じくらい大きく変わったのだと私は悟った。二人とも、もはや昨日までとは別人だった。
「レイ。これからどうしようか？」
「わかんねえ。あんたを病院には連れていけない。一人で行かせるわけにもいかない。どうすりゃいいんだ」
　彼のジレンマを解決しようと、私たちは話し合った。いくつもの可能性を検討して、どうすれば双方とも納得するかを考えた。私が案を出し、そのたびに彼が理由をつけて却下した。私はまた別の案を出す。彼は耳を傾け、考え、首を振り、また考え直した。私たちは少しずつ歩み寄っていった。
　やがて、お互いが納得できる取り引きが成立した。私は彼を逃がし、彼も私を逃がす。私は彼のことを誰にも言わないし、警察にも通報しないと約束した。ただし条件が一つ —— 彼がもう二度とこんなことをしないと約束すること。彼は約束した。そうするしかない。
　太陽が丘の向こうから顔を出すころ、私たちはふたたびバンに乗り込んだ。私が助手席に座り、レイが運転して、彼の知っている病院に向かった。彼が車を停めると、私は有り金全部と —— 200ドルほどあった —— 質屋で金に替えるようにと腕時計を二つばかり渡した。それから二人で一緒に通りを渡った。太陽がまぶしかった。朝早い時間だった

in the day but already warm. He had his army jacket and sleeping bag under one arm, his duffel bag slung over his shoulder. Somewhere in the bundle there was a black gun.

🎧 **150**

We shook hands. I smiled at him, and he continued to look confused. Then I said good-bye and walked away.

In the emergency room of L.A. County Hospital, a doctor scraped away small bits of metal, skin and hair, and ❶sewed stitches into my scalp. He asked me how it had happened, and I told him, "I was shot, four times."

🎧 **151**

"You're a lucky man," he said. "The two bullets that hit you both ❷glanced off your skull. You have to report this to the police, you know."

"Yes, I know," I said. I already knew that I was lucky, but even more, I felt ❸blessed. I didn't go to the police. I had made a promise and had received a promise in return. I kept my promise. I like to think that Ray kept his.

Lion Goodman
San Rafael, California

---

❶ sew: 〜を縫い合わせる　❷ glance off . . . : (弾丸などが)〜をかすめる　❸ blessed: 神の恵みを受けた

が、もう暑くなりはじめていた。彼はアーミージャケットと寝袋を片手でかかえ、ダッフルバッグを肩から下げていた。その荷物のどこかに、黒いピストルが入っているはずだった。

　私たちは握手した。私はにっこり笑ったが、彼はまだ狐につままれたような顔つきをしていた。私はさよならを言い、歩きだした。

　LA郡立病院の緊急治療室で、医者は私の頭から金属片や皮膚や髪をこそげるようにして取り除き、傷を縫い合わせた。どうしたのだと訊かれたので、「銃で4発撃たれました」と答えた。

　「あなたは運がいい」医者は言った。「4発のうち当たったのは2発で、どちらも頭蓋骨をかすめている。通報の義務はご存知ですね？」

　「ええ、わかっています」私は言った。自分が幸運なことはもうわかっている。それだけではない、神の恵みを一身に受けているのだ。私は警察に行かなかった。なぜなら私は約束し、その見返りに彼も約束をしたのだから。私は自分の約束を守った。レイもきっと守ってくれたと思いたい。

ライオン・グッドマン
カリフォルニア州サンラファエル

🎧 152-156

WAR

戦争

🎧 153

I THOUGHT MY FATHER WAS GOD

　These things happened in Oakland, California, at the end of World War II. I was six years old. I didn't know what war was then, but I was aware of some of its consequences. ❶Rationing, for one thing, since I had a ❷ration book with my name on it. My mother kept it for me, along with the ration books that belonged to my brothers. I remember the ❸blackout, the ❹air-raid warnings, and the sight of warplanes flying overhead. My father was a ❺tugboat captain, and I remember talk about ❻troopships, submarines, and ❼destroyers.

🎧 154

　I also remember my grandmother taking fat to the butcher shop to be ❽reclaimed and going downtown to the ❾federal building to toss aluminum scrap into the window ❿wells on the sidewalk side of the building.

🎧 155

　But what I remember most is Mr. Bernhauser. He was our backyard neighbor. He was especially ⓫mean and unfriendly to kids, but he was also rude to adults. He had an Italian plum tree that hung over the back fence. If the plums were on our side of the fence, we could pick them, but God help us if we got over the fence line. ⓬All hell would break loose. He would scream and yell

---

※トラック152をはじめ、オースターによる導入のナレーションのスクリプトは、232〜235ページにまとめて掲載されています。
❶rationing: 配給（制）　❷ration book: 配給手帳　❸blackout:（空襲などに備えた）灯火管制
❹air-raid warning: 空襲警報　❺tugboat: タグボート、引き船　❻troopship: 軍隊輸送船
❼destroyer: 駆逐艦　❽reclaim: 〜を再生利用する　❾federal building: 連邦政府ビル　❿well: 井戸状のへこんだ穴　⓫mean: 意地悪い　⓬all hell breaks loose: 大混乱に陥る、てんやわんやに

父さんは神様だと思った

　ここに記すのは第二次大戦の終わりごろ、カリフォルニア州オークランドで起こった出来事である。私は6歳だった。当時まだ私は戦争というものが何なのかわかっていなかったが、戦争によって起きたことにはいくつか気づいていた。たとえば配給、なぜなら自分の名前の入った配給手帳があったから。私の配給手帳は兄たちの分とまとめて母が保管していた。灯火管制、空襲警報、頭上を戦闘機が飛んでいく光景を覚えている。父はタグボートの船長で、軍隊輸送船や潜水艦や駆逐艦の話を聞いたことも覚えている。

　祖母が再利用のために脂肪を肉屋に持っていったこと、町の中心部にある連邦ビルまで出かけて行って、壁についていた投入口からアルミの切れ端を投げこんでいたことも覚えている。

　しかし一番強く記憶に残っているのはバーンハウザーさんのことだ。彼の家は我が家と裏庭同士で接していた。子供には特に意地悪で冷たい人だったが、大人に対しても無礼だった。彼の庭にはプルーンの木が1本あり、枝が柵越しにうちの庭に伸びていた。柵からこちら側になった実は採っても大丈夫だったが、柵の線を越えようものならさあ大変。とんでもない騒ぎになる。バーンハウザーさんは私たちに向かってわめき、

なる

at us until one of our parents came out to see what the ❶fuss was about. Usually it was my mother, but this time it was my father. No one liked Mr. Bernhauser very much, but my father was particularly against him because he kept all the toys and balls that had ever landed in his yard. So there was Mr. Bernhauser yelling at us to ❷get the hell out of his tree, and my father asked him what the problem was. Mr. Bernhauser took a deep breath and ❸launched into a ❹diatribe about thieving kids, breakers of rules, takers of fruit, and monsters in general. I guess my father ❺had had enough, for the next thing he did was shout at Mr. Bernhauser and tell him to ❻drop dead. Mr. Bernhauser stopped screaming, looked at my father, turned bright red, then purple, grabbed his chest, turned gray, and slowly ❼folded to the ground. I thought my father was God. That he could yell at a miserable old man and make him die ❽on command was beyond my comprehension.

🎧 156

I remember that Ray Hink lived across the street. We were in the same grade, and his grandmother lived upstairs. She was a tiny old woman who always wore a high-collar dress. She sat in the window with a pair of opera glasses and kept watch on the neighborhood. If we were good, she would let us look through the glasses and smell the rose petals she kept in an ❾alabaster jar on her table. She said that the rose petals were from Germany and the jar was from Greece. One afternoon, I was allowed to handle the precious glasses

---

❶fuss: 騒ぎ　❷get the hell out of . . . : 〜からとっとと出ていけ　❸launch into . . . : 〜を始める、やり出す　❹diatribe: 罵倒　❺have had enough: もうたくさん［うんざり］だと思う　❻drop dead: くたばっちまえ　❼fold:（人が）倒れる　❽on command: 命令に応じて　❾alabaster: アラバスター、雪花石膏

怒鳴り、父か母が何事かと出てくるまでやめないのだった。たいていは母だったが、この時は父だった。バーンハウザーさんを快く思う人はいなかったが、父はとりわけ反感を持っていた。何しろ、はずみで向こうの裏庭に入ったおもちゃやボールは、一つとして返してくれないのだから。さて、バーンハウザーさんはうちの木から降りろと私たちに叫んでいる最中で、どうしました、と父は尋ねた。バーンハウザーさんは大きく息を吸い込むと、とうとうと罵詈雑言をまくしたてた —— こそ泥のガキども、法律破り、果物泥棒、できそこないの化け物……。さすがに父も、堪忍袋の緒が切れたのだと思う。何とバーンハウザーさんに向かって、くたばれ、と怒鳴りつけたのだ。バーンハウザーさんはわめくのをやめて父を見つめ、顔を真っ赤にし、それから紫になり、胸をつかみ、今度は顔を土気色にしてゆっくりと地面にくずおれた。私は父さんは神様なんだと思った。父さんは気難しい老人を怒鳴りつけて、意のままに死なせられるのだ。それは私の理解を超えた出来事だった。

　通りをはさんだ向かいに、レイ・ヒンクという子が住んでいたのを覚えている。私たちは同じ学年で、レイのおばあさんはその家の2階に住んでいた。おばあさんは小柄な人で、いつも衿の高い服を着ていた。オペラグラスを持って窓際に座り、ご近所に目を光らせていた。私たちがいい子にしていると、オペラグラスをのぞかせてくれて、テーブルの上のアラバスターの壺に入れてあるバラの花びらの香りも嗅がせてくれた。花びらはドイツ製で壺はギリシア製だよ、とおばあさんは言った。ある午後のこと、私は大事なグラスを使うお許しをもらって外の通りを

and was looking out at the street. A cab ❶pulled up, and a tall, skinny sailor got out. He shook hands with the ❷cabby, who took a ❸sea bag from the trunk, and I knew that it was my Uncle Bill, home from the war. My grandmother came running down the steps into his arms. She was crying. I remember the stars that hung in the windows of some of our neighbors' houses. My grandmother told me it was because someone had lost a son in the war. I was glad that we didn't have any stars in our window. That night we had a huge celebration for Uncle Bill. I went to sleep feeling glad that my uncle was home safe. I didn't think about Mr. Bernhauser anymore.

Robert Winnie
Bonners Ferry, Idaho

---

❶ pull up: (車などが)止まる ❷ cabby: タクシーの運転手 ❸ sea bag: (引きひもで締める円筒状の)船員用のズック袋

眺めていた。タクシーが止まり、背の高い痩せっぽちの水兵が降りた。水兵は、トランクからキャンバス地の袋を取り出した運転手と握手した。私はその人がビルおじさんで、戦争から帰ってきたんだとわかった。祖母がうちの階段を駆け下りてきて、おじさんの腕の中に飛び込んだ。祖母は泣いていた。近所の家で何軒か、窓に星が下がっていたのを覚えている。戦争で息子さんを亡くした人がいるからだよ、と私は祖母に聞かされていた。うちの窓に星がなくてよかったと思った。その夜、私たちはビルおじさんの帰還を盛大に祝った。おじさんが無事に帰ってきたことを喜びながら私は眠りに落ちた。バーンハウザーさんのことはもう考えなかった。

ロバート・ウィニー
アイダホ州ボナーズフェリー

🎧 157-178

LOVE

愛

🎧 158

WHAT IF?

I received my ❶discharge papers on April 25, 1946. I had survived three years of army ❷service in World War II, and now I was heading home on a train to Newark, New Jersey. The last thing I'd done at the ❸base in ❹Fort Dix was to buy a white shirt at the ❺post exchange—a symbol of my return to civilian life.

🎧 159

I was eager to put my grand plan for the future into action. I would return to college, ❻launch my career, and look for the girl of my dreams. And I knew exactly who that girl would be. I'd ❼had a crush on her ever since high school. The question was: How could I find her? We hadn't been in contact for four years. Well, it might take some time, I thought, but find her I would.

🎧 160

When the train pulled into the station, I gathered up my bags, ❽tucked my new shirt under my arm, and headed down to the bus platform—the last ❾leg of my journey home. And then, miracle of miracles, there she was, just as I had remembered her: a short, slim, dark-haired ❿winsome beauty. I walked up to her and said hello, hoping she hadn't forgotten me. She hadn't. She threw her arms around my neck and kissed me on the cheek, telling me how glad she was to see me. Fortune was truly smiling on me, I thought.

※トラック157をはじめ、オースターによる導入のナレーションのスクリプトは、232〜235ページにまとめて掲載されています。
❶discharge: 除隊　❷service: 兵役　❸base: 基地　❹Fort Dix: フォート・ディクス（ニュージャージー州中南部にある軍用地および陸軍訓練センター）　❺post exchange:（駐屯地の）売店、販売部　❻launch:（事業・計画など）を始める、に着手する　❼have a crush on . . . : 〜に熱を上げている、のぼせている　❽tuck: 〜をしまい込む　❾leg:（旅行などの）一行程、一区切り　❿winsome: 人

もしも

　私は1946年4月25日に除隊書類を受けとった。第二次世界大戦において陸軍で3年の軍務を生き延び、ニュージャージー州ニューアークへ向かう列車で家に帰ろうとしていた。フォート・ディクス基地で一番最後にやったのは、駐屯地の売店で白いシャツを買うことだった。それが民間人の生活に戻ることの象徴だった。

　今後の大計画に早くとりかかりたくて、私はうずうずしていた。大学に復学し、仕事に乗りだし、理想の女の子を探すのだ。その子が誰だか、私にははっきりわかっていた。高校以来ずっとのぼせていた相手だ。問題は見つける方法である。4年間にわたり音信不通だったのだ。でも時間はかかっても絶対に見つける気だった。

　列車が駅に入ると私は荷物を集め、新しいシャツを脇にはさんで、階段を降りてバスの乗降場へと向かった。バスに乗れば、もう家だ。その瞬間、なんという奇跡、昔と変わらぬ彼女がそこにいたのだ。小柄でほっそりした、髪の黒い、魅力的な美人。私は寄っていって、忘れられていないよう願いつつ、こんにちはと声をかけた。彼女は忘れずにいてくれた。私の首に両腕をまわし、頬にキスをして、会えて嬉しいわと言ってくれた。運命の女神が本当に微笑みかけてくれていると思った。

を引きつける、魅力のある

🎧 161

It turned out that she had been on the same train, coming home for the weekend from ❶Rutgers University, where she was studying to be a teacher. The bus she was waiting for wasn't mine, but that didn't matter. I wasn't about to ❷let my opportunity slip away. We got on the same bus—hers—and sat together ❸reminiscing about the past and talking about the future. I told her of my plans and showed her the shirt I had bought—my first step toward making my dream come true. I didn't tell her that she was supposed to be step two.

🎧 162

She told me how lucky I was to have found that shirt, since men's civilian clothing was in such short supply. And then she said, "I hope my husband will be as lucky as you when he gets out of the navy next month." I got off at the next stop and never looked back. ❹Alas, my future was not on that bus.

🎧 163

Thirty-one years later, in 1977, I met her again at a high-school ❺reunion—not quite so dark-haired, not quite so slim, but still winsome. I told her that my career was going well, that I was married to a wonderful woman, and that I had three teenaged children. She told me that she was a grandmother several times over. I thought enough time had passed for me to mention that meeting three decades before—what it had meant to me, and how every de-

---

❶ Rutgers University: ラトガーズ大学（ニュージャージー州ニューブランズウィックにある州立大学）
❷ let ... slip away: ～をみすみす逃してしまう　❸ reminisce about ...: （過去の経験・出来事）を楽しく思い起こす　❹ alas: ああ、悲しや　❺ reunion: 同窓会

我々は同じ列車に乗っていたことがわかった。彼女は教師を目指してラトガーズ大学で勉強中で、週末を利用して家に帰るところだという。待つバスは違ったが、それはどうでもよかった。好機をみすみす逃す気はなかった。同じバスに乗り込んだ。彼女が待っていた方だ。並んで座って、思い出話にふけったり、将来について語りあったりした。私は今後の計画を語り、買ったシャツを見せた。夢を実現するための第一歩なんだ。二歩めは君だとは言わなかった。

　彼女は私に、そのシャツが見つかったのは幸運よ、男物の服はすごく不足しているから、と言った。そして、こう続けた。「夫が海軍を来月出るときも、あなたくらい運がいいといいな」。私は次の停留所で下車して、一度も振り返らなかった。嗚呼、わが未来はあのバスには乗っていなかったのだ。

　31年経った1977年に、高校のクラス会で彼女と再会した。前ほど髪は黒くなく、前ほどほっそりもしていなかったが、相変わらず魅力的だった。私は仕事が順調なこと、素晴らしい女性と結婚したこと、10代の子供が3人いることを話した。こっちはもう孫が何人もいるおばあちゃんよ、と彼女は言った。充分な時間が流れたのだから、30年前の出会いを話題にしてもいいだろうと思った。あの出来事が私にとってどれだけ意味があり、細部もすべて記憶にくっきり刻み込まれているという

tail of it was ❶etched in my memory.

🎧 164

    She looked at me ❷blankly. Then, putting a ❸coda to half a lifetime of "❹what ifs," she said, "I'm sorry, but I don't remember that at all."

Theodore Lustig
Morgantown, West Virginia

---

❶ etch: 〜をエッチングする、鮮明に焼きつける　❷ blankly: ぼかんとして、無表情に　❸ coda: コーダ、終結部（楽曲・楽章などの最終部分。曲が完了したことを強く印象づける部分）　❹ what if: もしもの話、仮定（疑問文の What if . . . ? ［〜としたらどうなるだろうか？］からきている）

ことを。
　彼女はぽかんとした表情でこちらを見た。そして、半生にわたるあまたの「もしも」に結尾(コーダ)をつける発言を行なった。「ごめんなさい、全然覚えてないわ」

シオドア・ラスティグ
ウェストヴァージニア州モーガンタウン

🎧 166

TABLE FOR TWO

In 1947, my mother, Deborah, was a twenty-one-year-old student at ❶New York University, ❷majoring in English literature. She was beautiful—❸fiery yet ❹introspective—with a great passion for books and ideas. She read ❺voraciously and hoped one day to become a writer.

🎧 167

My father, Joseph, was an ❻aspiring painter who supported himself by teaching art at a junior high school on the ❼West Side. On Saturdays, he would paint all day, either at home or in Central Park, and treat himself to a meal out. On the Saturday night in question, he chose a neighborhood restaurant called the Milky Way.

🎧 168

The Milky Way happened to be my mother's favorite restaurant, and that Saturday, after studying throughout the morning and early afternoon, she went there for dinner, carrying along a used copy of ❽Dickens's ❾*Great Expectations*. The restaurant was crowded, and she was given the last table. She settled in for an evening of ❿goulash, red wine, and Dickens—and quickly lost touch of what was going on around her.

---

❶New York University: ニューヨーク大学（ニューヨーク市にある米国最大級の私立大学） ❷major in . . . : 〜を専攻する　❸fiery: 情熱的な、激しやすい　❹introspective: 内省的な　❺voraciously: 貪欲に、旺盛に　❻aspiring:（aspiring . . . で）〜志望の人　❼West Side: ウェストサイド（マンハッタン西部の地区）　❽Dickens: ディケンズ（Charles Dickens。英国の小説家。1812-70）　❾*Great Expectations*:『大いなる遺産』（貧しい孤児 Pip を主人公とするディケンズの自伝的小説）　❿goulash: グーラーシュ（ハンガリーの料理で、牛肉とタマネギのパプリカ入りシチュー）

お二人席

　1947年、私の母デボラは21歳の大学生で、ニューヨーク大学で英文学を専攻していました。美人で、気性は烈しいけれど内省的で、本と思想に情熱を寄せていました。大の読書家で、いつか作家になりたいと思っていました。

　父ジョゼフは駆け出しの画家で、ウェストサイドの中学校で美術を教えて暮らしていました。土曜日は自宅かセントラルパークでひがな一日絵を描き、奮発して外食するのが習慣でした。問題の土曜の晩、ジョゼフは近所の〈ミルキー・ウェイ〉というレストランに行くことにしました。

　ミルキー・ウェイはたまたま母の大好きなレストランで、その土曜日の朝から午後半ばまでずっと勉強していた母は、ディケンズの『大いなる遺産』の古本を持って、夕飯を食べに行きました。レストランは混みあっており、母は最後の空きテーブルに案内されました。ハンガリー風ビーフシチュー、赤ワインとディケンズの夕べに身を落ち着けると、あっという間に周囲の様子は頭に入らなくなりました。

🎧 169

 Within half an hour, the restaurant was ❶standing-room-only. The ❷frazzled hostess came over and asked my mother if she would be willing to share her table with someone else. Barely glancing up from her book, my mother agreed.

🎧 170

 "A tragic life for poor dear Pip," my father said when he saw the ❸tattered cover of *Great Expectations*. My mother looked up at him, and at that moment, she recalls, she saw something strangely familiar in his eyes. Years later, when I begged her to tell me the story one more time, she sighed sweetly and said, "I saw myself in his eyes."

🎧 171

 My father, entirely ❹captivated by ❺the presence before him, swears ❻to this day that he heard a voice inside his head. "She is your destiny," the voice said, and immediately after that he felt a ❼tingling sensation that ran from the tips of his toes to the ❽crown of his head. Whatever it was that my parents saw or heard or felt that night, they both understood that something miraculous had happened.

🎧 172

 Like two old friends catching up after a long absence from one another, they talked for hours. Later on, when the evening was over, my mother wrote her telephone number on the inside cover

---

❶standing-room-only:（レストランや劇場で）満員　❷frazzled: 疲れ切った　❸tattered: ぼろぼろに傷んだ　❹captivate:〜の心を奪う、〜を魅惑する　❺the presence: 目の前に現われた人　❻to this day: 今日に至るまで　❼tingle: ぞくぞくさせる　❽crown: 頭のてっぺん、脳天

30分後、レストランは満員になりました。くたくたの女主人がやってきて、ご相席お願いできますかと訊ねました。本からほとんど目も離さずに、母は了承しました。
　「気の毒なピップの悲惨な人生」というのが、『大いなる遺産』のすりきれた表紙を見た父の第一声でした。母は父を見上げた瞬間、その瞳に不思議に懐かしいものを見たと追憶しています。何年も経ってから、またあのお話をしてとせがむと、母は愛らしい溜息をついて、こう言いました。「お父さんの目のなかに、自分が見えたのよ」
　父は眼前に現われた女性にすっかり魅了され、頭のなかで声がしたといまなお断言します。「これぞ運命の人」とその声が言った途端、つま先から頭のてっぺんまでぴりぴりと電気が走ったのです。その夜に両親が見たり、聞いたり、感じたりしたものが何であったにせよ、とにかく二人とも、何か奇跡的なことが起きたのだと理解していました。
　久しぶりに会った旧友のごとく、二人は何時間も語りあいました。やがて晩の終わりに、母は『大いなる遺産』の内表紙に電話番号を書いて、

of *Great Expectations* and gave the book to my father. He said goodbye to her, gently kissing her on the forehead, and then they walked off in opposite directions into the night.

🎧 173

Neither one of them was able to sleep. Even after she closed her eyes, my mother could see only one thing: my father's face. And my father, who could not stop thinking about her, stayed up all night painting my mother's portrait.

🎧 174

The next day, Sunday, he traveled out to Brooklyn to visit his parents. He brought along the book to read on the subway, but he was exhausted after a sleepless night and started feeling ❶drowsy after just a few paragraphs. So he slipped the book into the pocket of his coat—which he had put on the seat next to him—and closed his eyes. He didn't wake until the train stopped at ❷Brighton Beach, at the far edge of Brooklyn.

🎧 175

The train was ❸deserted by then, and when he opened his eyes and reached for his things, the coat was no longer there. Someone had stolen it, and because the book was in the pocket, the book was gone, too. Which meant that my mother's telephone number was also gone. In desperation, he began to search the train, looking under every seat, not only in his car but in the cars on either side of him. In his excitement over meeting Deborah, Joseph had foolishly

---

❶drowsy: 眠たい　❷Brighton Beach: ブライトンビーチ（ブルックリンの南端にある海岸）
❸deserted:（場所が）人けのない

父に本を渡しました。父は母の額にそっとおやすみの口づけをして、二人は夜のなかをそれぞれ反対の方向へ去っていきました。

　二人とも寝つけませんでした。目を閉じても、母の目に浮かぶものはひとつだけ。父の顔です。一方、父も父で母のことを片時も忘れられず、夜を徹して母の肖像を描きつづけました。

　翌日曜日、父は両親を訪ねにブルックリンへ向かいました。地下鉄で読もうと、あの本を持ってきてはいましたが、眠れぬ夜のせいでへとへとで、何段落かを読んだだけで眠たくなりました。そこで、隣の席に置いていたコートのポケットに本を滑り込ませて、目を閉じました。ようやく目覚めたのはブルックリンのはずれ、ブライトンビーチに列車が到着したあとでした。

　すでに列車に人影はなく、目を開けて持ち物に手をのばすと、コートがありませんでした。盗まれたのです。本はポケットに入れていましたから、本もありません。ということは、母の電話番号もなくなってしまったのです。父は車内を必死に捜し、座席の下も全部見ました。乗っていた車両だけでなく、前後の車両も見て回りました。デボラに出会えた興奮のあまり、ジョゼフは愚かにも彼女の名字を訊くことを怠ってい

❶neglected to find out her last name. The telephone number was his only link to her.

🎧 176

The call that my mother was expecting never came. My father went looking for her several times at the ❷NYU English Department, but he could never find her. Destiny had betrayed them both. What had seemed ❸inevitable that first night in the restaurant was apparently ❹not meant to be.

🎧 177

That summer, they both headed for Europe. My mother went to England to take literature courses at Oxford, and my father went to Paris to paint. In late July, with a three-day ❺break in her studies, my mother flew to Paris, determined to absorb as much culture as she possibly could in seventy-two hours. She carried along a new copy of *Great Expectations* on the trip. After the sad ❻business with my father, she hadn't had the heart to read it, but now, as she sat down in a crowded restaurant after a long day of sight-seeing, she opened it to the first page and started thinking about him again.

🎧 178

After reading a few sentences, she was interrupted by a ❼maître d' who asked her, first in French, then in broken English, if she wouldn't mind sharing her table. She agreed and then returned to her reading. A moment later, she heard a familiar voice.

"A tragic life for poor dear Pip," the voice said, and then she

---

❶neglect to . . . : 〜するのを怠る　❷NYU: = New York University　❸inevitable: 必然的な、運命的な　❹not meant to be: そうなる運命ではなかった　❺break: 休暇　❻business: 出来事　❼maître d': (レストランなどの)ボーイ長、ヘッドウェイター(= maître d' hôtel)

たのです。電話番号が唯一の絆でした。

　母が心待ちにしていた電話は、いつまでもかかってきませんでした。父は母を捜しにニューヨーク大学英文科に何度も出向きましたが、捜し当てられませんでした。運命が二人をともに裏切ったのです。レストランで初めて会った夜に必然と思えたことは、必然ではなかったようでした。

　その夏、二人はそれぞれヨーロッパへ発ちました。母はオックスフォードで文学の講義を受けにイギリスへ、父は絵を描きにパリへ行きました。7月末に母は3日間の休暇を利用して、パリへ飛びました。72時間のあいだに精一杯文化を吸収しようと心に決めていました。この旅行に『大いなる遺産』の新しい本を携えていました。父との悲しい一件があって以来読む気になれなかった作品でしたが、いままた、あちこち見て回った長い一日の終わりに、混みあうレストランに腰を落ち着け最初のページを開いて、改めてあの人を想いました。

　何行か読んだところで、ボーイ長の質問が割り込んできました。最初はフランス語、次にとぎれとぎれの英語で、相席よろしいですかと訊かれました。ええと答えて、読書を再開しました。すると聞き覚えのある声がしました。

　「気の毒なピップの悲惨な人生」と声は言い、見上げると、またあの人

looked up, and there he was again.

Lori Peikoff
Los Angeles, California

だったのです。

ロリー・パイコフ

カリフォルニア州ロサンゼルス

🎧 179-201

DEATH

死

🎧 180

I DIDN'T KNOW

My husband died suddenly at the age of thirty-four. The next year was filled with sadness. Being alone frightened me, and I felt hopelessly ❶insecure about my ability to raise my eight-year-old son without a father.

🎧 181

It was also the year of "I didn't know." The bank ❷levied a service charge on ❸checking accounts that went below five hundred dollars—I didn't know. My ❹life insurance was ❺term and not an ❻annuity—I didn't know. Groceries were expensive—I didn't know. I had always been protected, and now I seemed completely unprepared to handle life alone. I felt threatened on all levels by the things I didn't know.

🎧 182

In response to the high cost of groceries, I planted a garden in the spring. Then, in July, I bought a small ❼chest freezer, hoping it would help to keep the household food budget down. When the freezer arrived, I was given a warning. "Don't plug it in for a few hours," the deliveryman said. "The oil needs time to settle. If you plug it in too soon, you could blow a fuse or burn up the motor."

🎧 183

I hadn't known about oil and freezers, but I did know about

※トラック179をはじめ、オースターによる導入のナレーションのスクリプトは、232〜235ページにまとめて掲載されています。
❶insecure: 不安な、心配な　❷levy: 取り立てる、徴収する　❸checking account: 当座預金口座
❹life insurance: 生命保険　❺term: 期間（ここでは term insurance［期間保険、定期保険］のことを指している）　❻annuity: 年金（ここでは annuity insurance［年金保険］のことを指している）
❼chest freezer: チェストフリーザー、箱型冷凍庫（長持の形をした上開きドアの冷凍庫）

知らなかった

　私の夫は34歳で突然亡くなった。その後の1年は悲しみに満ちていた。一人でいるのはおそろしく、8歳の息子を父親なしで育てることにどうしようもない不安を感じていた。

　それは「知らなかった」続きの1年でもあった。銀行が預金額500ドル未満の当座預金口座から維持手数料を取ることを私は知らなかった。自分の生命保険が年金保険でなく定期保険であることを私は知らなかった。食料品が高いことも知らなかった。それまでずっと守られてきた私は、これから一人でやっていく準備がまったくできていないように思えた。あらゆる次元において、今まで知らなかったいろいろな事実に脅威を感じた。

　食料品が高価なので、私は春に菜園を始めた。それから7月には小さな冷凍庫を買った。これで食費が抑えられればと願ってのことだった。冷凍庫が届いた時に一つ注意を受けた。「まだ2、3時間は電源につながないでください」と配達の人は言った。「オイルが落ち着くのに時間がかかるんです。プラグを差し込むのが早すぎると、ヒューズが飛んだりモーターが焼き切れたりするおそれがあります」

　オイルや冷凍庫のことは知らなかったが、ヒューズを飛ばすことにつ

blowing fuses. Our little house, wired by a ❶demented electrician, blew lots of fuses.

🎧 184

Later that evening I went out to the garage to start up the freezer. I plugged it in. I stood back and waited. It ❷hummed to life with no blown fuses and no overheated motor. I left the garage and walked down the ❸drive to ❹soak in the soft, warm air. It was less than a year since my husband had died. I stood there in the ❺glow of my neighborhood, watching the lights of the city twinkling in the distance.

🎧 185

Suddenly—darkness, everywhere darkness. No lights burned in my house. There were no neighborhood lights, there were no city lights. As I turned around and looked into the garage, where I had just plugged in my little freezer, I heard myself say aloud, "Oh my God, I didn't know . . . " and an ❻audible bubble of ❼giddiness ❽escaped. Had I blown the fuses of a whole city by plugging in my freezer too soon? Was it possible? Had I done this?

🎧 186

I ran back to the house and turned on my battery-powered police-band radio. I heard sirens in the distance and feared they were coming to get me, "the widow lady with the freezer." Then I heard over the radio that a drunk driver had ❾taken out the breaker pole on the main road.

---

❶demented: 頭のおかしい　❷hum: ブーンという音を立てる　❸drive: (家へ通じる) 私道 (driveway)　❹soak in . . . : 〜につかる、浸る　❺glow: 輝き　❻audible: (声・音が) 聞こえる　❼giddiness: めまい　❽escape: 漏れる、流れ出る　❾take out . . . : 〜を壊す

いては知っていた。頭のおかしい電気屋が配線した小さな我が家では、しょっちゅうヒューズが飛んでいたのだ。

　その晩、時間がたってから、私は冷凍庫の電源を入れにガレージへ行った。プラグを電源に差し込み、一歩さがって様子を見た。冷凍庫はヒューズを飛ばすこともなく、モーターが過熱することもなく、ブーンという音とともに動き出した。ガレージを出て玄関までの道を歩きながら、私はやわらかくあたたかい空気に包まれた。夫が逝ってからまだ1年にもなっていなかった。私は近所の家の明かりを浴びて立ち、遠くでまたたく街の灯を見ていた。

　突然、真っ暗になった。どこもかしこも真っ暗だ。うちの明かりも、近所の家の明かりも、街の明かりも、全部消えた。くるっと振り返って小さな冷凍庫のプラグを差し込んだばかりのガレージをのぞきこむと、言葉が口から飛び出した。「まあ大変、知らなかった……」。めまいの泡が、音を立てて湧き出てきた。冷凍庫のプラグを早く入れすぎて、街じゅうのヒューズを飛ばしちゃったのかしら？　そんなことってありうる？　私のせいなの？

　私は家に駆け戻り、電池式の警察無線ラジオをつけた。遠くでサイレンが鳴り、私を、「冷凍庫の持ち主の未亡人」をつかまえにこちらに向かってきているのではないかと心配になった。その時、酔っ払った運転手が幹線道路のブレーカーのついた電柱を壊したことがラジオで報じられた。

🎧 187

　I was ❶overwhelmed by both relief and ❷embarrassment—relief because I hadn't caused the ❸blackout, and embarrassment because I'd thought that I could. Standing there in the darkness, I also felt something replace the fear that I had been living with since my husband's death. The feeling was somewhere between lightness and joy. I had ❹giggled at my ❺misplaced power, and at that moment I knew I had my humor back. I had lived a sorrowful and frightened year of "I didn't know." The sadness wasn't gone, but deep within myself, I could still laugh. The laughter made me feel powerful. After all, hadn't I just blacked out a whole city?

Linda Marine
Middleton, Wisconsin

---

❶ overwhelm:（人）を（精神的・感情的に）圧倒する　❷ embarrassment: 気恥ずかしさ、決まり悪さ　❸ blackout: 停電　❹ giggle: くすくす笑う　❺ misplaced: 見当違いの

安堵と恥ずかしさがどっと押し寄せた。停電が自分のせいではなかったということでほっとし、自分のせいかもしれないと思ったことが恥ずかしかった。そしてまた、その暗闇に立っていた時、何かがやってきて、夫が亡くなってからずっと抱えてきた不安にとってかわるのを私は感じた。軽やかさと喜びの中間くらいの何かだった。ばかみたいに自分の力を過大評価したことを思うと笑いがこみあげ、その瞬間、自分のユーモアが戻ってきたことに気がついた。その時まで私は、「知らなかった」づくしの悲しいびくびくした1年を過ごしていた。悲しみが消えはしなかったが、心の奥の深いところで私はまだ笑うことができる。笑うと力が湧いてきた。だって、たったいま街じゅうを停電させたじゃないの！

リンダ・マリーン
ウィスコンシン州ミドルトン

🎧 189

DRESS REHEARSAL

My mother had ❶been diagnosed with ❷congestive heart failure. The doctors said that she was too old and too sick to save and that they would "make her as comfortable as possible." No one knew how much time she had left: it could be days, weeks or months. She lived for seven more months, dying at eighty-nine.

🎧 190

We'd had a ❸rocky time together. She had never been easy to get along with, especially when I was a child. Maybe I wasn't easy, either. Finally, when I was forty-two years old, I gave up hoping she'd turn into the kind of mother I'd always wanted. On Christmas Eve, while visiting her and my father, I cut the ❹umbilical cord ❺at the top of my lungs. I stopped talking to her for a year and a half. Then, when we were back on speaking terms, I stuck to only the most ❻superficial subjects. This ❼sat very well with her; in fact, at one point she sent me a letter saying how glad she was that we had become so close.

🎧 191

The ❽retirement community she lived in was four hours away. When I got ❾word that she was dying, I started to spend a lot of time visiting her. The first month after she received her ❿prognosis, she was very depressed and ⓫distant. She either slept or stared at

---

❶be diagnosed with...: 〜と診断される　❷congestive heart failure: 鬱血性心不全　❸rocky: (人生などが)困難の多い　❹umbilical cord: へその緒(ここでは「母との関係」といった意味で比喩的に用いている)　❺at the top of one's lungs: 声を限りに　❻superficial: 取るに足らない　❼sit well with...: 〜に快く受け容れられる　❽retirement community: 退職者の居住施設　❾word: 消息、知らせ　❿prognosis: 予後(病気の経過および結末に対する見通し。特に回復の見込み)　⓫distant: よそよそしい

予行演習

　私の母は鬱血性心不全と診断されていた。医師たちは、治療するには高齢でもあるし病状も進んでいるから、「できるだけ快適に過ごせるようにしましょう」と言った。あとどれぐらいの時間が残されているのか誰にもわからなかった。数日かもしれないし、数週間かもしれないし、数カ月かもしれない。母はそれから7カ月生き、89歳で亡くなった。

　私と母はぶつかってばかりだった。母はどの時期をとっても一緒にいて楽な人物ではなく、私が子供の頃は特にそうだった。たぶん私も扱いやすい子供ではなかったのだろう。42歳の時、私はついに、母が自分がずっと求めていたような母親になってくれるという望みを捨てた。クリスマスで母と父を訪ねていたとき、イブの日に、私は声を限りに叫んで、母と私をつないでいたへその緒を切ったのだ。それから1年半の間私は母と口をきかなかった。その後また話をするようになった時には、本当にどうでもいいことしか話さないことにした。これは母には受けがよかった。実際、ある時母は手紙をよこし、こんなに距離が縮まってうれしいと書いてきた。

　母の住んでいる退職者のコミュニティーは、私の家から4時間の距離にあった。死期が迫っていると聞いて、私は頻繁に見舞いに行くようになった。宣告を受けてからの1カ月、母はとても落ち込んでいてよそよそしかった。眠っているか、黙ったまま悲しみに顔を仮面のようにして

the wall, silent, her face a mask of misery. She'd insisted on being ❶catheterized so she'd never have to get out of bed again, and then she'd settled down to the business of dying. One day during that month, I was sitting in the chair next to her bed. The sun had set and her room was almost completely dark. I shifted my chair closer and rested my elbows on the edge of her bed. She reached out her hand to touch my face and stroked it very gently. It was a wonderful thing.

🎧 192

During another visit a couple of weeks later, my mother experienced the first of the six little deaths that ❷preceded her real death. When I arrived, my father went out to do some errands. I was playing a game of ❸rummy with my mother, and she was ❹cheating like crazy, when she announced suddenly that she had to go to the bathroom. So I helped her out of bed and "❺spotted" her as she made her slow way to the toilet with her ❻walker. When we got into the tiny bathroom, she let out a long breath and collapsed. I caught her and lowered her to the floor. She was breathing the ❼agonized breaths of the dying and was unconscious, her eyes open but blank. I was paralyzed. She eventually let out a long final breath and didn't take another one in. I watched her face turn blue and her lips turn purple. Then I looked at the pulse on her neck, which was easy to do because she was so terribly skinny. As I watched, the pulse stopped. She was completely still. I held her there for a mo-

---

❶ catheterize: 〜にカテーテルを挿入する　❷ precede: 〜の前に起こる　❸ rummy: ラミー（トランプのゲームの一種）　❹ cheat like crazy: 無茶苦茶にインチキをする　❺ spot: 介助する（実際には母にはもうほとんど力がなく、ほぼ全面的に力を貸したので spotted にクォートが付いている）　❻ walker: 歩行器　❼ agonized: 苦しげな

壁を見つめているかだった。ベッドから出る必要がないようにカテーテルを入れてほしいと自分で主張し、それから死ぬ作業に取り掛かったのだった。そんなある日、私は母の枕元の椅子に座っていた。日は沈んで部屋はほとんど真っ暗だった。私は椅子を寄せてひじをベッドの端についた。母は手を伸ばして私の顔に触れ、すごく優しく撫でてくれた。すばらしい出来事だった。

　それから2週間ばかりして私が見舞いに行っていた間に、母は本当に亡くなる前に起きた6回の小さな死の第1回を経験した。私が着くと、父は何か用を足しに出かけた。私は母とラミーをして遊んでいて、母は猛烈にずるをしていた。と、母がいきなり、お手洗いに行きたいと言い出した。そこで私は母がベッドから出るのを手伝い、歩行器を使ってのろのろバスルームに向かうのを「介助」した。ちっぽけなバスルームに入ると、母はふうっと長い息を吐いて倒れこんだ。私は母を抱きとめて床に下ろした。母は死にかけている人間特有の苦しげな呼吸をしていて、意識がなく、目は開いていたがうつろだった。私は凍りついてしまった。やがて母はふうっと最後の息を吐いて、次の息を吸わなかった。その顔が青くなり、唇が紫になるのを私は見つめた。それから首の脈を診た。母は痛ましいほど痩せ細っていたから、脈を診るのは簡単だった。私が見守る中、脈は止まった。母はぴくりとも動かなかった。

ment, frozen. I asked her ❶out loud if she was dead; of course she didn't answer. I thought about what an honor it was that she had chosen me to die with, and then—oh no, oh no, oh no! I gently lowered her head to the floor and told her that I had to make a call and that I would be right back. I went to the phone and called the main desk. Then I went back into the bathroom and looked down at her. She seemed small and ❷forlorn. I sat on the floor behind her head, ❸hauled her into a half-sitting position, and held her in my arms for a few minutes, wondering how long it would take before someone got there.

🎧 193

All of a sudden, her body ❹jerked. I almost ❺jumped out of my skin. Then I thought: it's just her nervous system settling. A couple of minutes later, there was another big body jerk. Then the agonized breathing started up again.

🎧 194

I couldn't believe it: she was alive. I struggled to stop mourning and adjust to this new reality while she began ❻huffing and puffing, ❼flailing around, smashing her arms against the sink and wall. She was weeping and moaning. I tried to quiet her, telling her where she was. Finally, she came back to consciousness, the blankness left her eyes, and she saw that she was on the bathroom floor. I had pushed her walker into the corner, and she reached for it, saying, "Get me up! I have to get up!"

---

❶ out loud: 声に出して　❷ forlorn: みじめな、よるべない　❸ haul: 引っぱる　❹ jerk: 急激に動く（3行下で名詞としても使われている）　❺ jump out of one's skin: 心臓が飛び出るほど驚く　❻ huff and puff: はあはあ息をする　❼ flail around:（腕などを）激しく振り回す

私はしばし母を抱いたまま凍りついていた。母さん、死んだの？と声に出して聞いてみた。もちろん答えはなかった。私といる時に逝くことにしてくれたなんてすごく光栄だと考え、それから —— ああ大変、大変！　私は母の頭をそっと床に下ろし、電話しに行くけどすぐ戻ってくるからね、と言った。私は電話のところに行って、受付にかけた。そしてバスルームに戻り、母を見下ろした。母は小さく頼りなげに見えた。私は母の頭の後ろの床に座り込み、上体を半ば起こした姿勢まで母の体を持ち上げ、数分間母を腕に抱いて、いつになったら誰かきてくれるのだろうと考えていた。

　不意に母の体がびくっと動いた。私はぎょっとして跳び上がりそうになった。それから、ただの神経系の反応よ、と考えた。2、3分後、体はふたたび大きくびくりと動いた。そして苦しそうな呼吸が戻った。

　信じられなかった。母は生きている。私は母の死を悼むのをやめ、懸命にこの新しい現実に適応しようと努めた。母ははあはあ息をしはじめ、腕を振り回して流しや壁に打ちつけた。すすり泣き、うめき声をあげた。私は母をおちつかせようとして、ここがどこかを伝えようとした。そしてとうとう、母は意識を取り戻し、目のうつろさも消え、自分がバスルームの床に倒れていることに気がついた。私が隅に押しやってあった歩行器に母は手を伸ばし、「起こして！　起きなくちゃ！」と言った。

🎧 **195**

I said, "I can't get you up alone, Mom. People are on their way to help. Just stay still with me until they get here."

She ❶gave in and collapsed against me, breathing hard. Right then, the doorbell rang, and then the ❷resident nurse and the attendant from the front desk let themselves in, rushing to the bathroom, fully expecting to find my mother dead. But there we were on the floor, two living people, one holding the other. The three of us got my mother onto the toilet, cleaned her up, and put her back in bed. Ten minutes later, my mother was beating me in a game of rummy, cheating like crazy.

🎧 **196**

Later that day I was sitting on the edge of my mother's bed. I can only imagine how ❸stunned and exhausted I must have looked, because she said to me, "Now, dear, when I'm really dying—not one of these ❹dress rehearsals I seem to be having—but when I'm really going, I want you to know that I'll be kissing you all over!" Then she ❺fluttered her hands around my head. With love pouring from her eyes, she said, "Kiss! Kiss! Kiss! Kiss!"

I'd never seen her so full of joy.

🎧 **197**

The next day, I had to leave, even though I didn't want to. Just as I was walking out the door, the phone rang. It was Sister Pat, a nun who worked with the hospice organization that was caring for my

---

❶ give in: 屈する、従う ❷ resident: 常勤の ❸ stun: 〜をぼう然とさせる ❹ dress rehearsal: 舞台稽古、ドレスリハーサル（本番と同じ衣装、装置、照明の下で行なう） ❺ flutter: 〜をぱたぱた振る、ひらひらさせる

私は言った。「私一人じゃ起こせないわ。今助けが来るところなの。みんなが来るまでこうして静かにしていましょうね」
　母は折れてくれて、一気に体の力を抜いて私に寄りかかった。ぜいぜいと息が荒かった。と、呼び鈴が鳴り、常勤の看護師と受付係が入ってきてバスルームへ駆けつけた。彼らは母が死んだものと思い込んでいた。しかし床の上にいたのは二人の生きた人間で、一人がもう一人を抱えていた。私たちは三人がかりで母をトイレに座らせ、体をきれいにしてあげてからベッドに戻した。10分後、母はラミーで猛烈にずるをしながら私を負かしていた。
　その日、しばらくたってから、私は母のベッドの端に座っていた。自分ではわからなかったが、きっとさぞショックを受けて疲れきっているように見えたのだろう、母がこう言った。「ねえ、私が本当に死ぬ時には —— 今回のみたいな予行演習じゃなくてよ —— 本当に行ってしまう時には、あなたにキスの雨を降らせてるんだってことを覚えておいてね」。そして母は両手を私の頭のまわりでひらひらさせた。目から愛情をあふれさせて母は言った。「キス！　キス！　キス！　キス！」
　あんなに喜びに満ちた母を見たのは初めてだった。
　次の日、私は母のそばにいたかったが用事があって帰らねばならなかった。ちょうど出がけに電話が鳴った。電話の主はシスター・パット、母の入っているホスピス組織と組んで活動している修道女だった。

mother. She said that the nurse had told her what had happened to my mother and asked if I thought it would be a good idea for her to pay a visit. Since both my parents ❶shunned any open talk of God or spirituality, I said I didn't think so. But then I said I'd like to chat with her on the phone.

🎧 198

I told Sister Pat that my mother had made a complete ❷turnaround in the past twenty-four hours. I told her how my mother had been completely and ❸inconsolably miserable, and that now, after what had happened, she seemed happy and content. It was like night and day, I said.

🎧 199

There was a long pause. Then Sister Pat said, "Your mother is a very fortunate woman."

"Huh?" I said, thinking, She's dying—that's fortunate?

Sister Pat continued. In twenty years of working with dying people, she said, she had observed that the ones who had ❹"little deaths" were very peaceful for the rest of their lives. She said it was as if they had got to take a little ❺look-see and realized that there was nothing to be afraid of on the other side.

🎧 200

My mother and I had six more months after that. She had four more dress rehearsals and was proud of all of them. One time, I called her up, and when she got on the phone she said, "Guess

---

❶shun: 〜を避ける　❷turnaround:（態度・方針などの）180度の転換、転向　❸inconsolably: 慰めようもなく　❹"little deaths": 朗読では " を "quote" と読んで、比喩であることを強調している。　❺look-see: ざっと見渡すこと、視察

昨日のことを看護師から聞いたとシスター・パットは言い、いまお見舞いに行くのは得策かしら、と尋ねてきた。うちの両親は神だの精神性だのについて人前で話すことを断固として避ける人たちなので、私は彼女に、来てもらわない方がいいと思うと答えた。でも私自身がこのまま少し電話で話を聞いてもらえるとありがたいと伝えた。

　母の態度がこの24時間でがらりと変わったことを、私はシスター・パットに話した。どうしようもなく落ち込んでいて慰めようもなかったのが、あのことが起こってからはすごく明るくなって、安らかな気分でいるようなんです。まるで夜と昼みたいです、と私は言った。

　長い間があって、シスター・パットは言った。「お母さんはとても幸運な方だわ」

　「え？」私は言った。死にかけているというのに、幸運ですって？

　シスター・パットは続けた。死を前にした方々を相手に仕事をするようになってからの20年間に見てきたことなのだけれど、「小さい死」を経験した人たちはそれからの時間をとても穏やかな気持ちで過ごせるものなのです。まるで、ちょっとだけ死の世界をのぞいてみて、あの世をこわがる必要は全然ないのだと気がつくみたいなの。

　母と私はその後さらに6カ月をともに過ごすことができた。母はもう4回予行演習をして、それをひどく得意がった。ある時私が電話をかけ

what I did today?"

"What, Mom?" I asked.

"I died again!"

🎧 **201**

We never talked about much—just the weather, bits of news—but it didn't matter anymore. We lived in a little blue egg of light, and the love poured back and forth between us inside the egg. I finally got the mother I'd been waiting for.

Ellen Powell

South Burlington, Vermont

ると、電話口に出た母は言った。「今日私が何をしたと思う？」

「何をしたの？」私は聞いた。

「また死んだのよ！」

　二人でそんなにたくさん話をしたわけではない。天気のこと、最近起こったこと、それぐらいだ。でもそれはもうどうでもよかった。私たちは青い光に満ちた小さな卵の中にいたのだ。卵の中の二人の間を、あふれるほどの愛情が往き来した。私はついに、ずっと待ち望んでいた母親を手に入れたのだった。

エレン・パウエル
ヴァーモント州サウスバーリントン

🎧 202-208

DREAMS

夢

🎧203

HEAVEN

This happened to me when I was six years old. I'm now over seventy-five, but it's as fresh in my mind as if it happened just yesterday.

My sister Dotty was eight years older than I was, and she was responsible for taking care of me after school. She hated having to do this, but I loved going along with her when she visited her friends. One afternoon, Dotty had to go to another girl's apartment to do a homework assignment and ❶dutifully dragged me to the building and up three ❷flights of stairs. I knew that I was going to be bored. When they did homework in the kitchen, I was neglected in every way. The two of them would giggle and ignore me. They called me "❸brat" and "❹pest" and often teased me to tears.

🎧204

On that particular afternoon, I had nothing to do. After all, I was only six years old. I tried to get their attention, but they were hard at work and wouldn't look over at me. So I decided to ❺have a fit. I just lay down on the floor and started kicking my feet. I screamed, I banged, I made all the noise I could. The tenant in the apartment below couldn't tolerate the noise, and so she grabbed a stick and started banging on the ceiling. That frightened me, but I stubbornly continued to kick and scream. What a horrible noise I

※トラック202をはじめ、オースターによる導入のナレーションのスクリプトは、232〜235ページにまとめて掲載されています。
❶dutifully: 律儀に ❷flight: (一階分の) 階段 ❸brat: がき、チビ ❹pest: 厄介者 ❺have a fit: 癇癪を起こす

天国

　これはわたしが6歳のときの出来事です。今わたしは75を過ぎていますが、まるで昨日のことのようにはっきり覚えています。

　姉のドティは8つ上で、学校から帰ってくるとわたしのお守りをするのが役目でした。ドティはひどく嫌がりましたが、わたしは姉にくっついて、お友だちの家に一緒に行くのが大好きでした。ある日の午後、ドティはお友だちの家に宿題をやりに行くことになり、しぶしぶわたしを連れて、アパートの階段を3階まで上がっていきました。今日はきっと退屈するだろうな、とわたしは心の中で思いました。姉とそのお友だちが台所で宿題をやっているあいだ、いつもまるきり放っておかれるからです。姉たちはよく二人でくすくす笑い合って、わたしを無視しました。チビだ、みそっかすだとからかわれて、泣かされることもしょっちゅうでした。

　その日も、わたしは手持ち無沙汰でした。何しろまだ6歳でしたから、じっとしていることができません。なんとか姉たちの気を引こうとしましたが、二人とも宿題に夢中で、こちらを見向きもしてくれませんでした。そこで、癇癪を起こすことにしました。床にひっくり返って足をばたつかせ、キーキーわめいたり、床を手でばんばん叩いたり、出せる音はぜんぶ出しました。すると下の階に住んでいるおばさんがその騒ぎに怒って、棒で天井をどんどんつつきはじめました。わたしは怖くなりましたが、意地を張って、なおもばたばたキーキーを続けました。我なが

made. But my sister went on ignoring me, and she and her friend just laughed to show how little they cared about what I was doing. And the lady below, in her second-floor kitchen, kept banging up and screaming ❶at the top of her lungs. Finally, I stopped crying—out of pure ❷exhaustion—but the lady kept on banging against her ceiling. I could feel the vibrations in my body, and then I heard her scream: "I'm coming up! You'll be sorry when I get there!"

🎧 205

My sister and her friend panicked—and so did I. Dotty grabbed my hand, pulled me to the door, and opened it, listening to make sure that the woman wasn't on her way up to our ❸landing. "Shut up," she said to me, and then she gave me a pinch on the arm to make sure I'd behave. I was so scared, I was ❹whimpering, but she kept pinching my arm until I calmed down. As we stood there on the landing, listening for signs of the woman, I could feel Dotty's body shaking with fear. We couldn't leave the building by going down the stairs because that would have meant passing in front of the woman's door. Dotty was worried that she was waiting for us. The only way out was to go up the stairs.

🎧 206

She pulled me up to the fourth floor, to the fifth floor, to the sixth floor, and then we came to a steel door. Luckily for us, she was able to open it. We went out onto the roof of the building, but I didn't know this. I had never been on a roof before, and I didn't

---

❶at the top of one's lungs: 声を限りに　❷exhaustion: 疲労　❸landing:（階段の）踊り場
❹whimper: めそめそ泣く

ら、大変な騒々しさでした。それでも姉はわたしを無視して、あんたのやってることなんか全然気にしてないわよ、と言わんばかりに、お友だちと二人でくすくす笑い合っていました。2階のおばさんは、相変わらずキッチンの天井を棒でつつきながら、大声で何かわあわあどなっていました。そのうちに、わたしは声を出すのをあきらめました。本当に疲れてしまったからです。ところが下のおばさんは、天井をつつくのをやめません。振動が体に伝わって、おばさんがこう言うのが聞こえました──「今からそっちに行ってやる！　うんと思い知らせてやるよ！」

　姉とお友だちは青ざめました。もちろんわたしもです。ドティはわたしの手をひっぱって玄関まで行き、ドアを開けて、おばさんが上がってきはしまいかと耳を澄ましました。「声出すんじゃないよ」とわたしに言って、言うことをきかせるために腕をつねり上げました。わたしは怖くて怖くて泣きべそをかいていたのですが、姉があんまりいつまでもつねるので、涙もひっこんでしまいました。二人で踊り場に立って、おばさんが上がってくる足音に聞き耳を立てていると、姉の体が震えているのがわかりました。階段を下りて逃げるわけにはいきませんでした。それだと、おばさんの家の前を通らなければならないからです。きっと待ち構えているにちがいない、と姉は言いました。そうなると、上へのぼっていくより他ありませんでした。

　姉はわたしをひっぱって、4階、5階、6階と階段を上がっていき、やがて階段は鉄のドアの前で行き止まりになりました。さいわい、ドアは姉の力で開きました。出ると、そこはアパートの屋上でしたが、わたしにはそうとはわかりませんでした。屋上というものに上がったことがなかったので、そこが何なのか、わからなかったのです。それは見たこと

know where we were. I didn't know what this place was. I remember that we climbed over walls, running from one ❶rooftop to another. Then Dotty stopped at another steel door and opened it and guided me down the stairs to safety.

🎧 207

We stepped out onto the sidewalk of this strange ❷block. I don't know why, not even to this day, but when our feet touched the sidewalk, I thought we'd gone to heaven. I imagined that we were in heaven. I looked around and was amazed to see children jumping rope, just like we did, and that everything looked the same—except how could that be when this was heaven? When we turned the corner, I could see stores, and people going into them and out of them carrying bundles, and I was amazed. "So this is what heaven looks like," I said to my sister, but she wasn't listening. Every new block was more exciting to me than the last. I ❸figured we'd reached heaven by climbing up the stairs and crossing over the rooftops. I was so happy to be there, where children played like me. Then we turned one more corner, and we were on the block where we lived. "How did our street get up to heaven?" I asked my sister. But she didn't answer me. She just pulled me through the door of our building and said, "Shut up."

🎧 208

I kept this experience to myself for many years. It was my secret. I truly believed that I'd been to heaven. Only I couldn't understand

---

❶ rooftop: 屋根、屋上 ❷ block: 界隈（四つ角から四つ角までをいう） ❸ figure: 〜だと思う

もない場所でした。わたしたちは塀を乗り越え、屋上から屋上へ飛びうつりました。そしてドティが似たような鉄のドアを見つけてそれを開け、わたしを連れて、なんとか無事に下までおりることができました。

　外に出ると、そこは一度も来たことのない界隈でした。どうしてだか今でもわからないのですが、歩道に下りたとたん、わたしはそこが天国だと思い込んだのです。ああ、天国に来たんだ、と思いました。あたりを見回すと、驚いたことに、わたしたちと同じような子供たちが普通に縄跳びをしていて、何もかもが元いた世界と一緒でした。天国なのに何もかも一緒ということが、わたしには不思議でなりません。角を曲がると、お店が並んでいて、買い物袋をかかえた人が出たり入ったりしていました。わたしはますますびっくりしました。「天国ってこんなところだったんだね」と姉に言いましたが、姉は聞いていませんでした。四つ角を越えるたびに、驚きはますます大きくなりました。階段をのぼって屋上を飛び越えたせいで天国に来たんだ、そうわたしは思いました。自分と同じような子供たちが遊んでいるところだとわかって、嬉しくてしかたがありませんでした。そのうちに角をまた一つ曲がると、ひょいとわたしたちの家のある界隈に出ました。「どうしてうちの近所と天国がつながってるの？」と姉にたずねましたが、姉は返事をしませんでした。わたしをアパートの中にひっぱっていき、「いいから黙るのよ」と言いました。

　このことを、わたしはずっと誰にも話しませんでした。自分ひとりの胸に、大切にしまってきました。あれはたしかに天国だったと、心の底から信じていたのです。ただ、どうやって行けたのかはいつまでも謎で

how I'd gotten there—or how I'd found the way back to my house. This happened in the ❶Bronx. We lived on Vyse Avenue.

Grace Fichtelberg
Ranchos de Taos, New Mexico

❶ Bronx: ブロンクス(マンハッタン北方の区)

した──そして、どうして帰ってくることができたのかも。ブロンクスでの出来事です。家はヴァイズ・アベニューにありました。

グレース・フィクテルバーグ
ニューメキシコ州ランチョス・デ・タオス

🎧 209-238

MEDITATIONS

瞑想

🎧210

HOMELESS IN PRESCOTT, ARIZONA

　Last spring I made a major life change, ❶and I wasn't suffering from a midlife crisis. At fifty-seven I'm way beyond that. I decided I could not wait eight more years to retire, and I could not be a legal secretary for eight more years. I quit my job, sold my house, ❷furnishings, and car, gave my cat to my neighbor, and moved to Prescott, Arizona, a community of thirty thousand, ❸nestled in the Bradshaw Mountains with a fine library, community college, and a beautiful town square. I invested the ❹proceeds from selling everything and now I receive $315 a month in interest income. That is what I ❺live off of.

🎧211

　I am ❻anonymous. I am not on any government programs. I do not receive any kind of welfare, not even ❼food stamps. I do not eat at the ❽Salvation Army. I do not take ❾handouts. I am not dependent on anyone.

🎧212

　My base is downtown Prescott, where everything I need is within a ❿radius of a mile and a half—easy walking. To go farther ⓫afield, I take a bus that makes a circuit of the city each hour and costs $3.00 for a day pass. I have a ⓬post-office box—cost, $40.00 a year. The library is connected to the Internet, and I have an e-mail ad-

---

※トラック209をはじめ、オースターによる導入のナレーションのスクリプトは、232〜235ページにまとめて掲載されています。
（タイトル）Prescott: 地元では「プレスキット」と発音する　❶and: といっても、しかし　❷furnishings: 備えつけ家具　❸nestled in...: 〜に収まった　❹proceeds: 売上高、収入　❺live off of...: 〜に頼って生活する　❻anonymous: 匿名の　❼food stamp:（低所得者に対して連邦政府が発行する）食券、食料切符　❽Salvation Army: 救世軍（貧者の救済などの社会事業に携わる

アリゾナ州プレスコットのホームレス

　去年の春、私の人生は一大転機を迎えた。いわゆる中年の危機に苦しんだわけではない。もう57歳、とっくにその危機は乗り越えていた。停年まで8年も待っていられない、あと8年も弁護士秘書ではいられない、そう私は決心したのだ。仕事を辞め、家や家具や車を売り、猫を近所の人に譲って、アリゾナ州のプレスコットに移った。そこはブラッドショー山脈に抱かれた人口3万人ほどのコミュニティで、立派な図書館やコミュニティカレッジ、それに美しい広場がある。なにもかも売り払ったお金を投資した結果、月に315ドルの利子収入を得るようになった。それが私の生活資金だ。

　私は匿名の存在だ。いかなる政府事業にも私の名前は載っていない。どんな種類の福祉も、食料切符すらも受けていない。救世軍の教会で食事をとりもしない。施しも受けない。私は誰にも頼らずに生きている。

　私の基地はプレスコットのダウンタウンにある。必要なものはすべて2キロ半四方、楽に歩ける範囲内で手に入る。もっと遠出するときは、1時間おきに町を周回しているバスに乗る。その1日乗車券が3ドル。私書箱を借りているのが、年に40ドル。図書館にはインターネットがあり、私は自分のEメールアドレスも持っている。レンタルの収納ス

キリスト教団体）　❾handout: (貧困者などへの)施し物、お恵み　❿radius: 半径　⓫afield: 家から離れて、遠くへ　⓬post-office box: (郵便局の)私書箱

dress. My storage space costs $27.00 a month, and I have access to it twenty-four hours a day. I store my clothes, cosmetic and ❶hygiene supplies, a few kitchen items, and ❷paperwork there. I rent a ❸secluded corner of a backyard a block from my storage area for $25.00 a month. This is my bedroom, complete with ❹arctic tent, sleeping bag, mattress, and lantern. I wear a ❺sturdy pack with a water bottle, flashlight, and Walkman, ❻toiletries and rain gear.

🎧213

Yavapai College has an ❼Olympic-size pool and a women's locker room. I take college classes and have access to these facilities; cost, $35.00 a month. I go there every morning to perform my "toilet" and shower. I go to the ❽Laundromat with a small load of clothes whenever I need to; cost, $15.00 a month. Looking ❾presentable is the most important aspect of my new lifestyle. When I go to the library, nobody can guess I'm homeless. The library is my living room. I sit in a comfortable chair and read. I listen to beautiful music through the stereo system. I communicate with my daughter via e-mail and type letters on the word processor. I stay dry when it's wet outside. Unfortunately, the library does not have a television, but I've found a student lounge at the college that does. Most of the time I can watch ❿*The News Hour*, *Masterpiece Theater*, and *Mystery*. To further satisfy my cultural needs, I attend ⓫dress rehearsals at the local amateur theater company, free of charge.

---

❶ hygiene: 衛生　❷ paperwork: 事務書類　❸ secluded:（場所などが）人目につかない　❹ arctic: 極寒用の　❺ sturdy: 丈夫な　❻ toiletry:（石けん・歯磨きなどの）洗面用具　❼ Olympic-size: オリンピックサイズの（長さ50メートル、幅21メートル以上の公認プールについていう）　❽ Laundromat: コインランドリー　❾ presentable: 見苦しくない、体裁のよい　❿ *The News Hour, Masterpiece Theater, and Mystery*: いずれも米国PBS（公共放送サービス）のテレビ番組　⓫ dress rehearsal: 舞台稽古

ペースは月に27ドルで、24時間出し入れ可能。そこに衣服や化粧品、衛生用品、台所用品を少し、それに事務書類を預けてある。それから、収納スペースがあるところから四つ角ひとつ行った人目につかない裏庭の一画を借りていて、これが月に25ドル、わが寝室で、防寒用テント、寝袋、マットレス、ランタンも揃っている。いつも持ち歩いている丈夫なバックパックには、水筒と懐中電灯、それにウォークマン、洗面用具、雨具を入れてある。

　ヤヴァパイ・カレッジではオリンピックサイズの大きなプールと女性用ロッカーがある。私は授業を取っているので、こうした施設を使う権利があるのだ。月35ドル。毎朝出かけていって、「身支度」を済ませてシャワーを浴びる。必要に応じてコインランドリーに行き、これがだいたい月15ドル。見苦しくない外見を保つことは、この新たなライフスタイルの重要な要素だ。図書館に行く私を見ても、誰もホームレスだとは思わない。図書館はわがリビングルームだ。快適な椅子に身を沈め、読書にふける。備えつけられたステレオを使って美しい音楽に耳を傾ける。一人娘との連絡には、電子メールと、ワープロで打った手紙を使う。雨が降っても、私は屋根の下。あいにく図書館にはテレビがないが、そのうちにカレッジの学生用ラウンジに置いてあるのを見つけた。たいていの時間、ここで『ニュース・アワー』や『名作劇場』、『ミステリー』などを見ることができる。さらなる文化的要求を満たそうと、地元のアマチュア劇団の舞台稽古を観にいく。これはタダ。

🎧 214

Eating inexpensively and ❶nutritiously is my biggest challenge. My budget allows me to spend $200.00 a month for food. I have a ❷Coleman burner and an old-fashioned ❸percolator. I go to my storage space every morning and make coffee, pour it into my thermos, load my backpack, go to the park, and find a sunny spot to enjoy my coffee and listen to ❹*Morning Edition* on my Walkman. The park is my backyard. It's a beautiful place to hang out when the weather is ❺clement. I can lie on the grass and read and nap. The mature trees provide welcome shade when it's warm.

🎧 215

My new lifestyle has been comfortable and enjoyable so far because the weather in Prescott during the spring, summer, and fall has been delightful, though it did snow ❻Easter weekend. But I was prepared. I have a parka, boots, and gloves, all warm and waterproof.

🎧 216

Back to eating. The ❼Jack in the Box has four items that cost $1.00—❽Breakfast Jack, ❾Jumbo Jack, a chicken sandwich, and two beef tacos. After I enjoy my coffee in the park, I have a Breakfast Jack. There's a nutrition program at the adult center where I can eat a hearty lunch for $2.00. For dinner, back to the Jack in the Box. I buy fresh fruit and ❿veggies at ⓫Albertson's. Once in a while I go to the Pizza Hut—all you can eat for $4.49. When I return to

---

❶ nutritiously: きちんと栄養をとって　❷ Coleman burner: コールマン・バーナー（代表的なアウトドア製品）　❸ percolator: パーコレーター（濾過装置つきのコーヒー沸かし）　❹ *Morning Edition*:『モーニング・エディション』（米国 NPR のラジオ番組）❺ clement:（天候が）穏やかな、温暖な　❻ Easter: イースター、復活祭（の日）（春分後の最初の満月の次の日曜日）　❼ Jack in the Box: ジャックインザボックス（ファーストフード・レストランチェーン店）❽ Breakfast Jack:（商標）ブレックファースト・ジャック（サンドイッチ）　❾ Jumbo Jack:（商標）ジャンボ・ジャック（ハンバー

最大の難関は、安価で栄養のある食事をとることだ。食費には月に200ドルまでしか出せない。私はコールマン・バーナーと旧式のパーコレーターを持っている。毎朝、収納スペースに行ってコーヒーを沸かし、魔法瓶に注ぎ、バックパックに荷物を入れて公園に出かけ、日当たりのいい場所でコーヒーを楽しみながら、ウォークマンでラジオの『モーニング・エディション』を聴く。公園は私の裏庭だ。天気が穏やかな限りのんびり過ごすのにうってつけの場所だ。芝生に寝そべって本を読み、うたた寝する。暖かなときは、大木が心地よい日陰を提供してくれる。

　新しいライフスタイルはいまのところ快適で楽しい。プレスコットの天候は、春、夏、秋を通してずっと素晴らしかったのだ。イースターの週末には雪が降ったが、こっちも準備はできていた。パーカ、ブーツ、手袋、どれも暖かく防水である。

　食事の話に戻ろう。〈ジャックインザボックス〉へ行けば、1ドルで食べられる品が4つある。ブレックファースト・ジャック、ジャンボ・ジャック、チキンサンド、ビーフタコス二つ。私は公園でコーヒーを飲んだあと、ブレックファースト・ジャックを食べる。成人センターで栄養プログラムなるものをやっていて、2ドルでたっぷり昼食が食べられる。夕食は、またジャックインザボックス。新鮮な果物と野菜をアルバートソンの店で買う。ときどきは、ピザハットにも行く。4ドル49セントで食べ放題。夕方、収納スペースに戻って、コールマン・バーナー

ガー）　❿veggie: = vegetable　⓫Albertson's: アルバートソン（社）（フード・ドラッグコンビネーションストアを経営する会社）

my storage space in the evening, I make popcorn on my Coleman burner. I only drink water and coffee; other beverages are too expensive.

🎧217

I've discovered another way to have a different eating experience and to combine it with a cultural evening. There's an art gallery downtown, and the openings of the new shows are announced in the newspaper. Two weeks ago I put on my dress and ❶panty hose, went to the opening, enjoyed eating the snacks, and admired the paintings.

🎧218

I've let my hair grow long, and I tie it back in a ponytail like I did in ❷grade school. I no longer color it. I like the gray. I do not shave my legs or ❸underarms and do not polish my fingernails, wear mascara, foundation, ❹blush, or lipstick. The natural look costs nothing.

🎧219

I love going to college. This fall, I'm taking ❺ceramics, ❻chorale, and ❼cultural anthropology—❽for enrichment, not for ❾credit. I love reading all the books I want to but never had enough time for. I also have time to do absolutely nothing.

🎧220

Of course there are ❿negatives. I miss my friends from back home. Claudette, who works at the library, ⓫befriended me. She

---

❶panty hose: パンティーストッキング　❷grade school: 小学校　❸underarm: 脇の下　❹blush: 頬紅　❺ceramics:（単数扱いで）陶磁工芸　❻chorale: 合唱曲　❼cultural anthropology: 文化人類学　❽for enrichment: 教養をつけるために　❾credit: 単位　❿negative: 欠点、不利な点　⓫befriend: 〜の友［味方］になってくれる

でポップコーンを作る。飲むのは水とコーヒーだけ。それ以外の飲み物は高くて手が出ない。

　最近、別の食べ方と、それを文化的な夕べと結びつけるやり方を発見した。ダウンタウンには美術館があり、新しい展覧会が開かれるときは新聞に告知が出る。2週間前、私はドレスを着てストッキングをはいてオープニングに出かけ、軽食を楽しみ、心ゆくまで絵画を眺めた。

　髪の毛は伸びるにまかせ、小学校のときのようにポニーテールに束ねている。もう染めることもしない。白髪が気に入っているのだ。足や脇の下のムダ毛処理はしなくなったし、爪を磨いたり、マスカラやファンデーション、頬紅や口紅もやめた。自然な外見は一銭もかからない。

　カレッジに行くのは好きだ。この秋は、陶芸、合唱、文化人類学のクラスを取っている。単位のためではなく、心を豊かにするためだ。いままでずっと読みたかったのに時間がなかった本を読むのもすごく楽しい。それに、まるっきり何もしない時間もちゃんとある。

　もちろん、この生活には不都合な点がいくつかある。故郷の友人たちと会えないのは寂しい。でも、図書館勤めのクローデットが友だちになってくれた。彼女は地元紙の特別記者だったことがあって、人々から

was a ❶feature writer for the local newspaper and is ❷adept at getting information from people. Eventually, I told her who I was and how I live. She never pressures me to live differently, and I know she's there for me if I need her.

🎧221

I also miss my Simon cat. I keep hoping that a cat will come my way, particularly before winter ❸sets in. It would be nice to sleep and ❹snuggle with a furry body.

🎧222

I hope I can survive the winter. I've been told that Prescott can have lots of snow and long stretches of freezing temperatures. I don't know what I'll do if I get sick. I'm generally an ❺optimist, but I do worry. Pray for me.

B. C.

Prescott, Arizona

---

❶ feature:（新聞・雑誌などの）特別［特集］記事　❷ adept at . . . : 〜がうまい　❸ set in:（悪天候などが）始まる　❹ snuggle: 寄り添う、すり寄る　❺ optimist: 楽天家、楽天主義者

情報を引き出す達人だ。やがて私は、自分が何者なのか、どのように暮らしているのかを彼女に話した。彼女は一度も私に、そんな生き方はやめなさいと迫ったりしない。そして私が彼女を必要とするときには、きっとそこにいてくれることを私は知っている。

　猫のサイモンと会えないのも寂しい。何とかして、冬が始まる前に猫が現われないかなといつも思っている。ふわふわした毛で覆われた体と一緒に寝たり寄り添ったりするのは、きっと素敵だろう。

　どうか、この冬を生き延びられますように。冬のプレスコットは雪がたくさん降ることもあり、凍えるほどの寒さが長いあいだ続くという。病気になったらどうしたらいいかもわからない。たいていのことには楽観的な私だが、それでもやっぱり心配だ。どうか、私のために祈ってください。

B・C
アリゾナ州プレスコット

🎧224

AN AVERAGE SADNESS

It is with small shame that I move to turn on the radio today. Radio is the friend I usually neglect; the friend I only think to ❶call upon when life has turned sad and desperate. I always return to it ❷flushed with guilt—but it is always waiting for me; it is always ready to take me back.

🎧225

When I first lived alone, I listened, like so many, each day: when I awoke in the mornings, and again in the evenings, when I returned from work. While I ❸waited out the ❹siege of my first New York summer, radio's sounds were the only ones I could ❺tolerate.

🎧226

And so, when my first relationship went bad, I found myself in an apartment ❻steeped in brown, and again I turned on the radio. The taste of ❼yucca, which I fried for the first time in that tiny kitchen, the smell of ❽smoke-saturated curtains and Murphy's Oil Soap, the interviews, the news reports, the long ❾recitation of member stations in the ❿Berkshires—these are bound to each other and to me, they are the taste, the smell, the ⓫sodden air of that ⓬isolation.

🎧227

Radio was made for the lonely, after all, ⓭the displaced and ⓮the

---

❶call upon...:（人）を（ちょっと）訪ねる　❷flushed with guilt: やましさを抱えて　❸wait out...:（嵐・危機など）が過ぎるのを待つ　❹siege:（災厄・悩みの）長く苦しい期間　❺tolerate: 〜に我慢する、耐える　❻steeped in...: 〜に染まった　❼yucca: ユッカ、イトラン（ニューメキシコ州の州花）　❽smoke-saturated: 煙の染み込んだ　❾recitation: 唱えるように話すこと　❿Berkshires: バークシャーヒルズ（= Berkshire Hills）（マサチューセッツ州西部のリゾート地）　⓫sodden: 湿っぽい　⓬isolation: 孤独、孤立状態　⓭the displaced:（戦争・被災などによる）難民、

ありきたりな悲しみ

　今日、ちょっとした気まずさを感じながら、私はラジオをつけようと向き直る。普段は気にも留めない友人、それがラジオだ。人生が悲しみと絶望に変わってしまったときにだけ、やましい思いに苛まれつつ、私は決まってラジオに戻っていく。でも、ラジオはいつも待っていてくれる。いつもふたたび私を受け容れてくれる。

　一人暮らしをはじめたころは、たいていの人たちと同じに、毎日ラジオを聴いたものだった。朝起きて聴き、夜仕事から帰るとまた聴いた。はじめて経験するニューヨークの夏の猛威が過ぎ去るのを待っているあいだ、唯一我慢できたのがラジオの音だった。

　だから、初めての恋愛が上手くいかなくなったときも、茶色で統一したアパートの自室で、ふたたびラジオのスイッチを入れた。その小さなキッチンで初めて揚げたユッカの味、タバコの煙が染み込んだカーテン、マーフィー社のオイルソープの臭い、インタビュー、ニュース、バークシャーヒルズの系列ラジオ局の名を長々と列挙するアナウンス。これらがたがいにつながりあい、私につながっている。それらはその孤独の味であり、匂いであり、湿った空気だ。

　結局のところ、ラジオは孤独な人たち、よるべない人、世界との接触

（より一般的に）よるべない人々　⓮ the out of touch: 社会とのつながりを失った者たち

out of touch. Unlike television—which stares stubbornly in a single direction, which demands the attention of the whole ❶battered body—radio is everywhere. Single people need radio, for only it can fill the enormous empty spaces that even their smallest apartments ❷harbor. It does not ❸spite us for our ❹distraction, but ❺tactfully begins from the moment we switch it on.

🎧228

Its sound is our ❻guardian angel; ❼ubiquitous but ❽unassuming. We move about our business while radio patiently follows. Its ❾persistence ❿soothes even our most sudden and ⓫sharp-edged isolations, softens the spaces between our souls and the ever-distant walls.

In these ways, radio is ⓬forgiving, and the lonely are in need of forgiveness.

🎧229

Last spring it seemed my whole life abandoned me—a needed job ⓭fell through, my relationship failed. I took the first, smallest, ⓮dingiest apartment that offered itself. I didn't have the patience, or the courage, to look further. I switched perfumes. I listened to the radio. And words started to drop in on me without warning.

🎧230

As I ⓯shivered in the rush of possibility, my comforts and routines ⓰wrestled away from me; I became aware of the air nearest to me. This air knew my skin, it was warm with my own voice. ⓱Shel-

---

❶battered: やつれた、虐待された　❷harbor: 〜を内部に持つ、抱え込む　❸spite: 〜に意地悪をする　❹distraction: 注意散漫、上の空　❺tactfully: 巧みに、つつましく　❻guardian angel: 守護天使　❼ubiquitous: 遍在する　❽unassuming: 偉ぶらない　❾persistence: 粘り強さ　❿soothe:（痛み・苦痛など）を和らげる、軽くする　⓫sharp-edged: 痛烈な　⓬forgiving: 寛大な　⓭fall through: 無駄に終わる、実現されずに終わる　⓮dingy:（場所が）みすぼらしい　⓯shiver: 身震いする　⓰wrestle away . . . : 〜を奪う　⓱shelter: 〜を保護する

をなくした人々のために作られたのだ。テレビは頑固に同じ方向だけを見つめていて、疲れはてた体全体の反応を要求する。それとは違い、ラジオはどこにでもいる。独り者にはラジオが必要だ。どんなにちっぽけな部屋にも漂う大きな空虚を埋められるのはラジオだけなのだ。ラジオは私たちの気がよそに散っても怒らないし、スイッチを入れた瞬間からつつましく関係を再開してくれる。

　ラジオの音は私たちの守護天使だ。遍在しつつも慎み深い。我々があれこれ用事を足して動き回るなか、我慢強くついて来てくれる。その粘り強さが、どんなに突然で辛い孤独も慰めてくれる。私たちの心と、遠く離れた壁との隔たりをそれは和らげてくれる。

　こんなふうにラジオは寛大であり、孤独な人たちには寛大さが必要なのだ。

　今年の春、私は人生からすっかり見捨てられた気分だった。必要としていた仕事はお流れになり、恋人とも別れた。部屋探しをはじめて最初に見せられた、最高にちっぽけでみすぼらしい部屋を借りた。それ以上探す忍耐も気力もなかったのだ。私は香水を変えた。ラジオを聴いた。すると、何の前兆もなしに、私のもとに言葉がやって来るようになった。

　押し寄せてくる可能性に震えるなか、日々の安楽や決まりきった仕事が私から離れていき、私は自分に一番身近な空気を意識するようになった。この空気は私の肌を知っていた。私自身の声を帯びて暖かかった。

tered, I grew still. I lifted plain and shining words from the cold that ❶braced my insides. They swam to me, they offered themselves to my net.

🎧231

For months I lived like this, avoiding new friendships, neglecting the few that had survived my prior ❷couplehood. I postponed getting a new job, preferring to ❸subsist on coffee, on toast, on the sun that would ❹brave my ❺filthy windows. These days were ❻indulgent and ❼untenable—I would have to find work, I would have to revive old friendships, I would have to form new ones. The harvest would fall off.

🎧232

Though I cried myself to sleep each night, this time was as sweet and as ❽thick as any I ever lived. Each moment I ❾distilled and drank off ❿at my leisure; each day I ⓫reaffirmed my greed for my own ⓬uninterrupted time, and only radio was invited.

I grew strong, alone like that. But slowly, practicality ended my ⓭respite. I moved in with a friend, I took a job. I fell in love.

🎧233

Falling in love is like ⓮painting yourself into a corner. Thrilled by the color you've laid down around you, you forget about freedom shrinking at your back. Neglected, my river slowed, my catches grew meager. I stopped listening to the radio. I once again began to think of time alone as something to spend or ⓯will away, rather

---

❶brace: 〜をしっかり押さえる［つかむ］　❷couplehood:（男女が）カップルを形成していること、2人の生活　❸subsist on . . . :（特にわずかな金や食糧）で生きていく　❹brave: 〜をものともしない　❺filthy: 汚い　❻indulgent: 寛大な、大目に見る　❼untenable: 支えきれない、持ちこたえられない　❽thick: 濃密な　❾distill: 〜を蒸留する　❿at one's leisure: 気ままに　⓫reaffirm: 〜を再び主張する　⓬uninterrupted: 誰にも邪魔されない　⓭respite:（仕事・苦痛などの）一時的中断　⓮paint oneself into a corner: 抜きさしならぬ羽目に自らを追い込む　⓯will away: 〜を意志

守られながら、私はまったく動かなくなった。私の内側を引きしめる冷たさから、私は簡潔で輝く言葉たちを引き揚げた。それらの言葉がこちらに泳いできて、私の網にひっかかる。

　数カ月というもの、私はそんなふうに暮らしていた。新しい友人関係を避け、前の恋人と一緒だった時期のあとにもかろうじて残った数人の親友とも連絡をとらなかった。新しい仕事を探すのも先延ばしにし、コーヒーとトースト、我が家の汚れた窓をものともしない太陽を糧に生きていた。気ままな、いつまでもやっていけるはずのない日々だった。仕事は見つける必要があったし、旧交を暖め、新たな友人関係を築かなくてはいけなかった。このままでは何もかもなくなってしまう。

　毎晩泣きながら眠っていたけれど、それはこの上なく甘く、濃密な時間だった。私はそれぞれの瞬間瞬間を気ままに蒸留し、飲みほした。日々、誰にも邪魔されない自分一人の時間を自分が欲していることをあらためて感じた。私に招かれるのはラジオだけだった。

　そんなふうにして、一人でいても私はだんだん強くなっていった。しかし、ゆっくりと、現実が私の一時休暇に終止符を打った。私は友人と同居し、仕事に就いた。恋に落ちた。

　恋をすることは、抜きさしならぬ場に自分を好きこのんで追い込むことだ。自分のまわりに塗りつけた色の鮮やかさにうち震えて、背後で小さくなっていく自由のことは忘れてしまう。顧みられなくなって、私の川の流れは遅くなり、水揚げも乏しくなっていった。私はラジオを聴かなくなった。またしても私は、一人の時間を、ゆったり体をのばせる場としてではなく、あくまで消費すべき、あるいは意志の力で消滅させる

の力でなくしてしまう

than something I could stretch myself across.

🎧234

And now, now that I have forgotten, things prepare themselves to ❶fall away again—another love will leave; I will take an apartment by myself. I feel the air turn ❷crisp, the walls ❸edge farther from my body.

🎧235

Shivering, nervous, I turn on the radio, for the first time in months. Paul Auster is reading a story about a girl who lost her father, who dragged a Christmas tree down the streets of a midnight Brooklyn. He's asking us for our stories.

There are conditions: that they be both brief and true.

🎧236

But I have no deaths, no travels worth repeating. I have no ❹strokes of wild fortune or ❺incredible tragedy. I have only an average sadness. Worse, I have been unable to write for weeks now, my mind ❻riddled instead by ❼imminent departures, imminent change.

🎧237

Then it strikes me: this moment is the friendly hand of solitude. The radio is inviting me back, back to the rooms it will fill with its voice of warmest flannel, back to the warm light of time spent alone.

---

❶fall away:（物が）崩れていく　❷crisp:（空気が）身の引き締まるような、冷たい　❸edge: 少しずつ進む　❹stroke:（幸運などの）一撃　❺incredible: 信じがたいような　❻riddled by . . .: 〜だらけで　❼imminent:（悪いことが）今にも起ころうとしている、切迫した

べき時間として考えはじめた。

　そしていま、私が忘れてしまったいま、ものごとはふたたび崩れていく準備を進めている。恋人はまた去っていくだろう。私は一人で部屋を借りることになるだろう。空気が冷えていき、壁が私の体からじりじり離れていくように感じられる。

　体を震わせ、落ち着かぬ思いで、何カ月かぶりに、私はラジオをつける。父親をなくして、クリスマスツリーを引きずって真夜中のブルックリンの街を歩く少女の物語をポール・オースターが朗読している。私たちの物語を送ってほしいとオースターは言っている。

　条件がある。短い、本当に起きた話でなくてはならない。

　でも、私には、くり返し語るに足る死も旅もない。突拍子もない運命や、信じられないほどの悲劇に襲われたこともない。私にはありきたりな悲しみしかない。もっと悪いことに、私は何週間も書けずにいる。頭は目先で起こりそうな離別や変化にかかずらわっている。

　と、私は思いあたる。いまこの瞬間は、孤独がさしのべる友好の手なのだ。ラジオは私を呼び戻している ── この上なく暖かいフランネルの声に満ちた部屋へと、一人で過ごす時間の暖かい光へと。

🎧 **238**

I have recognized the invitation only as I have written these lines. This is my story, complete with the climax that is now.

Sometimes it is good fortune to be abandoned. While we are looking after our losses, our selves may slip back inside.

Ameni Rozsa

Williamstown, Massachusetts

この文章を書きながら、やっと私はその呼ぶ声に気がついた。これが私の物語なのだ。そこにはクライマックスもちゃんとある。いまこの瞬間がそうだ。
　ときには、うち捨てられるのも幸運なことなのだ。喪失から立ち直っているあいだに、自分がいつの間にか戻ってくるかもしれないのだから。

アメニ・ローザ
マサチューセッツ州ウィリアムズタウン

Spoken Introductions to the Stories
「イントロダクション」とそれぞれの話の前に収録された、オースターによる作品紹介のトランスクリプションと対訳です。

🎧001（p. 12）INTRODUCTION
Harper Audio presents I Thought My Father Was God: And Other True Tales from NPR's National Story Project. Edited, introduced and read by Paul Auster.

🎧022（p. 44）ANIMALS
The first section of stories is "Animals." And the very first one in this section is called "The Chicken," and it's written by Linda Elegant of Portland, Oregon.

🎧024（p. 46）ANIMALS
This story is entitled "Vertigo" by Janet Zupan of Missoula, Montana.

🎧038（p. 60）OBJECTS
The title of this story is "A Bicycle Story," and it's written by Edith Riemer of Cherry Valley, New York.

🎧048（p. 70）OBJECTS
"The Striped Pen" by Robert M. Rock of Santa Rosa, California.

🎧054（p. 78）FAMILIES
The next section of stories comes under the heading of "Families," and the first one I'm going to read is entitled "Rainout" by Stan Benkoski of Sunnyvale, California.

🎧059（p. 82）FAMILIES
"Taking Leave" by Joe Miceli of Auburn, New York.

🎧092（p. 108）SLAPSTICK
"A Felt Fedora" by Joan Wilkins Stone of Goldendale, Washington.

🎧097（p. 112）SLAPSTICK
This story is entitled "Bronx Cheer," and it's written by Joe Rizzo of the Bronx, New York.

🎧0109（p. 122）STRANGERS
The next section of stories is entitled "Strangers." "Dancing on Seventy-fourth Street, Manhattan, August 1962" by Catherine Austin Alexander of Seattle, Washington.

イントロダクション
ハーパー・オーディオが贈る、『父さんは神様だと思った　NPR〈ナショナル・ストーリー・プロジェクト〉実話集』。編集、イントロダクション、朗読、ポール・オースター。

動物
第一部のテーマは『動物』です。筆頭の物語は「鶏」、著者はオレゴン州ポートランド在住のリンダ・エレガント。

動物
次の話は、モンタナ州ミズーラのジャネット・ズーパンによる「ヴァーティゴ」です。

物
次の物語のタイトルは「自転車物語」、著者はニューヨーク州チェリー・ヴァレーのイーディス・ライマー。

物
「縞の万年筆」、カリフォルニア州サンタローザ、ロバート・M・ロック。

家族
次の部は『家族』という範疇に収まる物語で、まず読むのは「雨天中止」です。著者はカリフォルニア州サニーヴェイル在住、スタン・ベンコスキー。

家族
「別れを告げる」、ニューヨーク州オーバーン、ジョー・ミセリ。

スラップスティック
「フェルトの中折れ帽」、ワシントン州ゴールデンデール、ジョーン・ウィルキンズ・ストーン。

スラップスティック
次の物語は、「ブロンクス流どたばた」。ニューヨーク州ブロンクス、ジョー・リゾ。

見知らぬ隣人
次のセクションのタイトルは『見知らぬ隣人』です。
「74丁目のダンス――1962年8月、マンハッタン」、著者はワシントン州シアトル在住、キャサリン・オースティン・アレグザンダー。

🎧 114 (p. 126) STRANGERS
"A Shot in the Light" by Lion Goodman of San Rafael, California.

🎧 152 (p. 156) WAR
"I Thought My Father Was God" by Robert Winnie of Bonners Ferry, Idaho.

🎧 157 (p. 164) LOVE
"What If?" by Theodore Lustig of Morgantown, West Virginia.

🎧 165 (p. 170) LOVE
"Table for Two" by Lori Peikoff of Los Angeles, California.

🎧 179 (p. 182) DEATH
"I Didn't Know" by Linda Marine of Middleton, Wisconsin.

🎧 188 (p. 188) DEATH
This story, written by Ellen Powell of South Burlington, Vermont, is entitled "Dress Rehearsal."

🎧 202 (p. 202) DREAMS
"Heaven" by Grace Fichtelberg of Ranchos de Taos, New Mexico.

🎧 209 (p. 212) MEDITATIONS
This next one was written by a woman who identifies herself as B.C. from Prescott, Arizona, and the title is "Homeless in Prescott, Arizona."

🎧 223 (p. 222) MEDITATIONS
"An Average Sadness" by Ameni Rozsa of Williamstown, Massachusetts.

見知らぬ隣人
「怪我の『光明』」、カリフォルニア州サンラファエル、ライオン・グッドマン。

戦争
「父さんは神様だと思った」、アイダホ州ボナーズフェリー、ロバート・ウィニー。

愛
「もしも」、ウェストヴァージニア州モーガンタウン、シオドア・ラスティグ。

愛
「お二人席」、カリフォルニア州ロサンゼルス、ロリー・パイコフ。

死
「知らなかった」、ウィスコンシン州ミドルトン、リンダ・マリーン。

死
次は、ヴァーモント州サウスバーリントン、エレン・パウエルによる、「予行演習」と題した物語です。

夢
「天国」、ニューメキシコ州ランチョス・デ・タオス、グレース・フィクテルバーグ。

瞑想
次の話の書き手は、アリゾナ州プレスコットに住むB.C.と名乗る女性で、題は「アリゾナ州プレスコットのホームレス」。

瞑想
「ありきたりの悲しみ」、マサチューセッツ州ウィリアムズタウン、アメニ・ローザ。

What's "Paul Auster Reads the National Story Project"?
『ポール・オースターが朗読するナショナル・ストーリー・プロジェクト』とは?

- アメリカの人気作家ポール・オースターがホストを務めたラジオ番組 National Story Project に投稿された物語をまとめた原書、I Thought My Father Was God: And Other True Tales from NPR's National Story Project から、監訳者の柴田元幸氏が18篇を選定しました。

- 本書には18篇分の英文、翻訳が収載され、オースターの朗読音声を無料ダウンロードできます。
  ※原書に掲載された180話全話の翻訳は新潮社より『ナショナル・ストーリー・プロジェクト』として刊行されています。

- 「イントロダクション」と各物語の前にオースターによる紹介が収録されています。紹介の英文と翻訳は232〜235ページにまとめて掲載されています。

I THOUGHT MY FATHER WAS GOD by Paul Auster

Copyright© 2001 by Paul Auster
All rights reserved.
Reprinted in English by permission of Henry Holt and Company, New York through Tuttle-Mori Agency, Inc., Tokyo

18 stories taken from I THOUGHT MY FATHER WAS GOD by Paul Auster
Japanese translation and English reprint rights arranged with Paul Auster c/o Carol Mann Agency, New York through Tuttle-Mori Agency, Inc., Tokyo

I THOUGHT MY FATHER WAS GOD by Paul Auster
Copyright© 2001 by Paul Auster
English language digital audio recording rights arranged with HarperCollins Publishers, New York, New York through Tuttle-Mori Agency, Inc., Tokyo.
All rights reserved.

Editor／編者紹介

ポール・オースター　Paul Auster
1947年ニュージャージー州生まれ。コロンビア大学大学院を中退後、フランスに渡り、別荘管理人など、さまざまな仕事に従事。帰国後、詩の創作や翻訳に携わったのち、「ニューヨーク三部作」で一躍小説界の表舞台に躍り出る。読みやすい文章のなかに哲学的要素などを組み込んだ秀作を次々と発表し、本国アメリカをはじめとしてフランス、日本など海外にも多くの読者を持つ希代のストーリーテラー。

Translators／訳者紹介

柴田元幸　Motoyuki Shibata
1954年東京都生まれ。東京大学名誉教授。著書に『翻訳教室』『アメリカン・ナルシス』『ケンブリッジ・サーカス』、村上春樹との共著に『本当の翻訳の話をしよう』などがある。本書掲載の作家以外にも、スティーヴ・エリクソン(『ゼロヴィル』)、マーク・トウェイン(『ハックルベリー・フィンの冒けん』)、ジャック・ロンドン(『火を熾す』)など、現代・古典の多数の作家作品を翻訳。雑誌『MONKEY』責任編集。本書ではAnimals、Objectsの章の翻訳と監訳を務めた。

岸本佐知子　Sachiko Kishimoto
翻訳者。訳書に『掃除婦のための手引き書』(ルシア・ベルリン著／講談社)、『話の終わり』(リディア・デイヴィス著、作品社)、『最初の悪い男』(ミランダ・ジュライ著／新潮社)、『セミ』(ショーン・タン著、河出書房新社)ほか。編訳書に『変愛小説集』『楽しい夜』(以上 講談社)ほか。著書に『ひみつのしつもん』『ねにもつタイプ』(以上 筑摩書房)ほか。本書ではStrangers、Dreamsの章を担当。

畔柳和代　Kazuyo Kuroyanagi
1967年生まれ。東京医科歯科大学教授。訳書に『空腹の技法』(ポール・オースター著／新潮文庫　柴田元幸と共訳)、『マン・オン・ワイヤー』(フィリップ・プティ著／白揚社)、『オリクスとクレイク』(M・アトウッド著／早川書房)、『秘密の花園』(F・H・バーネット著／新潮文庫)、『サンタクロース少年の冒険』(L・フランク・ボーム著／新潮文庫)ほか。本書ではFamilies、Loveの章を担当。

前山佳朱彦
1972年生まれ。翻訳者。訳書に『エドガー@サイプラス』(アストロ・テラー著／文藝春秋)、『サロン・ドット・コム　現代英語作家ガイド』(ローラ・ミラー編、共訳／研究社)。本書ではSlapstick、Meditationsの章を担当。2005年逝去。

山崎暁子　Akiko Yamazaki
1972年生まれ。法政大学文学部准教授。訳書に『火山の下』(マルカム・ラウリー著、共訳／白水社)、『ヒア・アンド・ナウ　往復書簡2008‐2011』(ポール・オースター、J・M・クッツェー著、共訳／岩波書店)、『渇湖』(ジャネット・フレイム著／白水社)ほか。本書ではWar、Deathの章を担当。

新装版

ポール・オースターが朗読する
ナショナル・ストーリー・プロジェクト

2019年12月13日　初版発行

編：ポール・オースター
訳：柴田元幸／岸本佐知子／畔柳和代／前山佳朱彦／山崎暁子
編集：株式会社アルク 出版編集部
AD：松田行正+杉本聖士
DTP：株式会社秀文社
印刷所：シナノ印刷株式会社

発行者：田中伸明
発行所：株式会社アルク
〒102-0073　東京都千代田区九段北4-2-6　市ヶ谷ビル
TEL：03-3556-5501
FAX：03-3556-1370
Email：csss@alc.co.jp
Website：https://www.alc.co.jp/

・落丁本、乱丁本は弊社にてお取り換えいたしております。
・アルクお客様センター（電話：03-3556-5501　受付時間：平日9時〜17時）
　までご相談ください。
・本書の全部または一部の無断転載を禁じます。
・著作権法上で認められた場合を除いて、本書からのコピーを禁じます。
・定価はカバーに表示してあります。
・ご購入いただいた書籍の最新サポート情報は、
　以下の「製品サポート」ページでご提供いたします。
　製品サポート：https://www.alc.co.jp/usersupport/
・とくに断りのない限り、
　本書に掲載の情報は2019年12月現在のものです。

© Motoyuki Shibata, Sachiko Kishimoto, Kazuyo Kuroyanagi,
Kazuhiko Maeyama, Akiko Yamazaki 2005, Printed in Japan

PC：7019061　ISBN：978-4-7574-3388-5　C0098